MW01041113

"Table for…
the Sun Up Café.

"Just me," M

coffee and cinnamon rolls made her stomach growl.

"Mind if I join you?"

Merry looked up from her menu and blinked. "Grady?"

Grady didn't wait for an invitation. He smiled at Merry as he sat down next to her.

Merry's heart thumped wildly in her chest and her stomach turned over. Was that butterflies or hunger? "What are you doing here?"

Grady shrugged, picked up Merry's menu and perused it. "Breakfast."

"No, I mean what are you doing *here*? At this restaurant."

He set the menu down and leaned his arms on the table. "A guy gets tired of the continental breakfast fare at the hotel. Robin suggested this place, said it's your favorite."

She studied Grady's face, trying to figure out why he would drive all the way up to Belford for breakfast, Robin's recommendation notwithstanding. Had he hoped to run into her or was he just bored with the hotel fare? She didn't know him well enough to figure that out. As Grady poured them both coffee, she could have sworn his eyes twinkled. *Stop it, Merry. You're not a lovesick schoolgirl.*

"You seem like a nice man. But just to be clear, I hate the idea of a corporate takeover of any public school, and you work for the one that's commandeering mine."

He winked at her. "Duly noted."

She took a breath and managed a smile. "But we do have Robin and Eli."

Grady smiled back. "If you ask me, that's a lot."

Praise for Pamela Woods-Jackson

"I enjoyed it! It [SUGAR COOKIES FOR BOXING DAY] is very charming."

~Robert Woods, author

~*~

"SUGAR COOKIES FOR BOXING DAY is a holiday romance filled with the sounds and smells of Christmas. It is delightful company and includes the recipe for the heroine's popular cookies."

~Lee Wilson, author

~*~

"I loved it!!!! I'm an aficionado of Hallmark movies. I could exactly picture this as one."

~J. Paul Burroughs, author

~*~

CERTAINLY SENSIBLE won the Literary Classics Seal of Approval, 2016.

"This author is going on my must-read list."

~ Theresa Joseph

~*~

"Endearing to the core! CONFESSIONS OF A TEENAGE PSYCHIC is a great read for anyone looking to reminisce about the days of high school…"
"Caryn has a strong voice; I like her."

~ Barbara Shoup, author

Sugar Cookies for Boxing Day

by

Pamela Woods-Jackson

Christmas Cookies Series

This is a work of fiction. Names, characters, places, and incidents are either the product of the author's imagination or are used fictitiously, and any resemblance to actual persons living or dead, business establishments, events, or locales, is entirely coincidental.

Sugar Cookies for Boxing Day

COPYRIGHT © 2022 by Pamela J Jackson

All rights reserved. No part of this book may be used or reproduced in any manner whatsoever without written permission of the author or The Wild Rose Press, Inc. except in the case of brief quotations embodied in critical articles or reviews.
Contact Information: info@thewildrosepress.com

Cover Art by *The Wild Rose Press, Inc.*

The Wild Rose Press, Inc.
PO Box 708
Adams Basin, NY 14410-0708
Visit us at www.thewildrosepress.com

Publishing History
First Edition, 2022
Trade Paperback ISBN 978-1-5092-4194-1
Digital ISBN 978-1-5092-4193-4

Christmas Cookies Series
Published in the United States of America

Dedication

In loving memory of my grandmother Charlotte Hall, whose cookie recipe inspired this story.

Chapter One
Wednesday, December 19

"Another end-of-semester Christmas party here at Belford Prep is in the books." Merry smiled at her friend and coworker.

"Mind if I have one of these?" Donna didn't wait for an answer but reached for a Santa-shaped sugar cookie, topped with red and green sprinkles.

"Help yourself." Merry took inventory of the mess in her classroom. The kids had swarmed in like locusts. They ate most of her homemade cookies, polished off the fruit juice, and tossed empty plates and cups into the trash can, causing refuse to spill out onto the surrounding floor. She removed the few remaining cookies from the paper plate atop her lecture podium, wrapped them in a Christmas napkin, and stuffed them into her well-worn, brown leather briefcase.

"I shouldn't eat this cookie." Donna pointed to her hips. "But they're so good and I'm surprised you have any left."

Merry smoothed down the navy-blue pantsuit that accentuated her tall, slender frame, crossed her classroom to the hall door, and peered out.

Thomas Belford Preparatory High School might have been empty of students, but the hall didn't look any better than Merry's classroom. Overflowing trash bins were everywhere, filled with discarded wrapping paper, dirty holiday-themed paper cups and plates, sticky candy cane wrappers, and of course the typical end-of-school-day trash—wadded notebook paper, torn folders, broken writing utensils. Someone had tossed an algebra textbook in the water fountain, and the *Happy Holidays* banner the PTA moms made now hung askew from the ceiling.

Merry shook her head and returned to her desk, perusing her open laptop. "Seems the Christmas party was a hit."

Donna nodded as she polished off the last bite of sugar cookie and dusted off her hands. "Got any plans tonight?"

"Not really." Merry hit Send on the email and closed her laptop. "My daughter and I talked about dinner, but she hasn't gotten back to me."

"Too busy with that new boy toy?" Donna's eyes twinkled as she leaned her elbows on Merry's desk.

Merry still had mixed emotions about her daughter's sudden engagement to a young man she'd only known a few months, and their headlong rush toward a summer wedding, but she pushed them aside. "She's just plain busy."

"Since Robin is," Donna put up air quotes, "'busy,' let's do something. You and me. Classes are done, it's Christmas break, and we need to get out and celebrate."

Merry lifted an eyebrow. "You're an art teacher. You haven't exactly been under a lot of pressure to give exams and turn in grades."

Donna sniffed. "I gave final exams just like you did." She put her hands on her ample hips and tapped a foot. "Okay, so I assigned projects, but I still had to grade them."

The overhead lights flickered off and then on again. Merry and Donna both looked up at the ceiling and then exchanged glances, but neither commented on the one-hundred-year-old school building's state of disrepair. Despite being in the ritzy town of Belford, Indiana, a suburb of Indianapolis, Belford Prep was the school district's red-headed stepchild.

Merry blew an errant lock of bangs out of her face. "I really should go home and get to bed early, since I still have to finish grading these essays and post my grades online tomorrow."

"Merry Halliday, you're not so old you have to go to bed with the chickens." Donna waggled a finger. "Tomorrow is teacher work day. No kids, so you've got the whole day to finish."

Merry eyed the stack of ungraded student essays on her desk. "Don't forget the faculty meeting Dr. Alexander's been reminding us all week. That'll eat into my work time."

Donna waved that away. "The principal's probably just handing out recognition awards, and it'll be quick and painless."

Somehow Merry didn't think that was the case, given the declining student enrollment, lack of money for basic supplies, and the building's state of disrepair. She sighed and gathered the essays, opened her briefcase, and stuffed them in.

"Come on, let's go out tonight." Donna poked her friend's shoulder. "You have to eat, you know."

Merry rubbed her arm where Donna jabbed her. She turned around and surveyed her white board, which was covered in black, red, and blue ink, rereading her instructions on writing the final essay on *A Christmas*

Carol the students spent nearly a month reading. She reached for the dry eraser and swiped at it, but like everything else in this school, the white board was old, and the ink just smeared into a pinkish mess. The board would require some spray cleaner and a soft cloth.

Every December she instructed her students to read the Charles Dickens' classic, a tradition she'd started when she was both a newlywed and a new teacher. She loved the story, loved Christmas, and especially loved the day after Christmas, or anyway, she used to. Boxing Day, as they called it in Canada and England, a holiday Americans didn't celebrate. She wasn't Canadian or British, of course, but her family always treated her birthday on December twenty-sixth like an extension of the holiday.

This year she almost changed her mind about teaching the Dickens novella because of the memories it stirred up. Yes, she'd been a widow for three years, long enough to face the reality of life without Bert, but somehow this year felt different because of her looming birthday. She dreaded facing that milestone alone.

Merry always loved literature. In college in the 1970s, she'd admired the handsome, sophomore English professor—okay had a crush on him, just like all the other girls did. She hung on his every word, but Robert Halliday kept his professional distance. A lovesick nineteen-year-old was off limits for a young professor hoping for tenure. Still, his aloof attitude hadn't stopped her from daydreaming about him and hoping for a way to attract his attention.

Merry remembered Professor Halliday's last lecture before classes dismissed for the holiday break that sophomore year. He'd assigned *A Christmas Carol.*

She'd giggled along with the other students as the professor arrived in class dressed as Charles Dickens and sat enthralled as he read aloud a scene as if he were the author. Looking back now, Merry knew that was when she started to fall in love with Bert. They began dating as soon as she graduated and married soon after.

But ever since Bert's death, teaching *A Christmas Carol* was just one more painful reminder of their life together.

"Hello? Where'd you go?" Donna waved a hand in front of Merry's face.

"Sorry." Merry took one more look at the smeared white board. "Just thinking about grading these essays."

Donna rolled her eyes. "All you do is go straight home from work every night, eat dinner alone, watch old holiday movies on TV, and go to bed early. Not tonight. It's time to start some new traditions."

Start some new traditions. After all these years, what would that even look like? The proverbial other shoe was about to drop on December twenty-sixth, so maybe a new start was overdue. "Since I seem to be free and I don't feel like cooking, I suppose I can spare an hour for dinner." Merry slipped into her suit jacket, picked up her briefcase, and prepared to follow Donna out the door, just as the lights flickered off, on again, and then off.

****

Merry exhaled a breath of cold air as she juggled her briefcase with one hand and dug in her handbag for her condo's front door key with the other. "Success!" She waved the key over her head in victory, but that was only half the battle. Without her glasses and in the waning light of a late December afternoon, she had to shove aside the Halloween ghost still hanging on the door handle and feel around to find the lock before inserting the key.

Normally, Merry removed her Halloween decorations the first of November, and by Thanksgiving her Christmas decorations were up. *Running a little late this year.* She had new next-door-neighbors and didn't want them to think she was one of those lazy people who left up holiday decorations year-round. She took down the skeleton, hurried inside, opened the coat closet, and tossed it in. "See you next year!" She dropped her briefcase and handbag by the front door, and flung her overcoat on the edge of the apartment-sized sofa.

"Spookie?" Merry called out. "Here, kitty! You hungry?" She glanced around, but the cat was nowhere to be seen. A one-bedroom condo didn't have too many places a cat could hide. Not like the three-thousand square foot home where she and Bert raised Robin. But a year ago, when its memories and size became too burdensome, Merry decided to downsize. After a short house-hunt, she found this condo in the perfect location for just the right price. It earned Robin's approval, and she was sure Bert would have approved, as well.

"Here, kitty." She looked under the coffee table, behind the TV opposite the sofa, and stepped into the adjacent kitchen. Merry shrugged and popped open a can of cat food. Spookie's bowl had been licked clean, and the cat usually came running at the sound of food being opened.

Merry...

What? Chills went down her spine, her eyes wide as she took a quick glance around. "Who's there?" She inched her way toward the bedroom, flipping on the hall light and then the bedroom overhead light.

"Meow, meow."

Spookie appeared at her feet, rubbing against her legs. Merry exhaled and lowered the bat. She had no idea where the cat had been hiding, but she berated herself for her overactive imagination. "Hey, kitty, you gave me a fright." She reached down and scratched the cat's ears.

Merry hadn't adopted Spookie so much as the cat had adopted her. On her first Halloween in the new condo last year, Merry opened the door to trick-or-treaters, and the most gorgeous black cat waltzed inside as if she owned the place. Merry inquired of the children and their parents if they knew whose cat she was, but no one did. Merry did her due diligence by hanging fliers around the condominium complex and posting notices on online missing pet sites. No one claimed her.

The vet judged Spookie to be about two years old, so after she was spayed and given a clean bill of health, Merry kept her. Or more accurately, Spookie condescended to stay.

Merry's phone rang, and she rushed from the hallway to the sofa to dig it out of her handbag. "Hello?"

"Mom?"

"Robin, I'm glad you called. I just had the weirdest experience." Merry was about to relate the whole cat calling her name story but thought better of it. Robin would think her mother was going senile mere days before her sixtieth birthday.

"I got your email," Robin said. "I know we talked

about dinner once you were done with classes, but Eli has a client appreciation Christmas party tonight. He says he needs me to be there."

"It's okay, hon. My plans changed anyway." Merry could picture Robin breathing a sigh of relief. She set the phone on the kitchen counter and put it on speaker while she finished dishing out the cat food.

"You sure?"

"I'm sure. Donna and I are going out for an early supper tonight, and I have papers to grade. I won't starve or pine away from loneliness." She set Spookie's dish back on the floor.

"How about if you meet Eli and me tomorrow night instead? His dad is in town on business. He's divorced you know."

Merry rolled her eyes, glad her daughter couldn't see that immature response. "If that's an offer for a fixup, I'll pass."

"We think you two would hit it off."

Merry barely knew her daughter's fiancé, and had only heard bits and pieces about his family. According to Robin, Eli's father was a handsome man in his late fifties, probably a playboy type if Merry had to guess. "I'd love to have dinner with you and Eli, and I'm willing to meet Eli's father, but only as parents of the future Mr. and Mrs. Williams."

"I'm keeping my maiden name," Robin said.

She opened her mouth to argue but decided to let it go. Her thirty-two-year-old daughter was happy with her slightly younger man, so Merry told herself she'd go along with whatever name she chose. "That's fine, Robin. Your father would be pleased."

"So I'll text you about dinner with Eli and his dad.

I gotta go. Love you." Robin disconnected.

She patted Spookie's head and glanced at the clock. Donna would be here soon, and she wanted to change out of her work clothes. She walked past the bathroom on the way to the bedroom and nearly tripped over Bert's Teacher of the Year plaque lying on the floor in the middle of the hallway. "How did this get here?" She lifted an eyebrow at the cat, but Spookie ignored her while she licked her feet.

Merry peered at the spot on the wall where the framed plaque had been hanging just this morning. Had Spookie jumped up and knocked it to the floor? Even a cat wasn't that agile. Or maybe the neighbors turned up their music so loud the wall vibrations knocked it off? That didn't seem likely, either. She picked up the plaque, checked to make sure it hadn't been damaged, turned it over, and found the problem—a broken hook on the back of the frame. She'd have to get it repaired.

Or would she? What if she just put it away and bought a new picture? The plaque had been important to Bert, but maybe she needed to try the new traditions thing Donna kept nagging her about. She studied the empty wall space and decided a framed landscape would look nice there.

She opened her bedroom closet and perused her wardrobe options, which were limited because of her overflowing laundry hamper. She and Donna would probably go to their favorite Chinese restaurant, so her comfortable, loose-fitting jeans, what Robin called her Mom jeans, would be fine. At least they were clean. She carefully hung up the pantsuit she'd worn all day and chose the ugly red Christmas sweater, with its decorated tree and Merry Christmas lettering woven in.

The doorbell rang as she gave her too long, chin-length, graying auburn hair one last swipe. She hurried out of the bedroom and opened the front door.

"Donna! Why are you dressed like that?" Merry motioned her friend inside.

"Thought I'd dress up in my date-night clothes." Donna glanced down at her form-fitting jeans and wool-lined, sleeveless puffy vest. "Why are you dressed like that?" She tsk-tsked at Merry's attire and reached down to stroke the cat. "Hey, Pookie."

"Spookie." Merry gave her well-worn sweater a self-conscious tug as she addressed the cat. "Be good, young lady."

Spookie grumbled but curled up on the sofa for a nap.

Merry retrieved her coat from the sofa and slipped into it. "You didn't explain your outfit."

"You didn't explain yours." Donna winked. "Never mind. I'm driving."

Merry's stomach growled long and loud. "Hong Kong Heaven?" She locked her front door and followed Donna to her car, parked in one of the condominium's visitor pads.

Donna clicked open both doors of her mid-sized sedan. She fastened her seatbelt, nodded as Merry did the same, checked her rearview mirror, and backed out of the parking space. But instead of turning right toward Hong Kong Heaven, Donna turned left onto the highway entrance ramp.

Merry gave Donna a quizzical look and opened her mouth to object.

With her focus still on the road, Donna reached over and adjusted the volume on the radio, blasting

Christmas carols.

Merry shrugged and settled in. After a twenty-minute drive past several exits, all of which led to perfectly good restaurants, she was out of patience. "Donna, I'm starved. Are we there yet?"

"You sound like one of the kids." Donna turned down the radio's volume, put on her signal, and exited the freeway. She eventually made a left-hand turn into the parking lot of a popular sports bar in Indianapolis, one already teeming with cars. She circled the lot several times before snagging a spot in the last row. "I guess you didn't check your text messages this afternoon," Donna said as they walked toward the entrance.

"I heard something ping while I was driving home, but I thought it was Robin." Merry directed a pointed look at her friend. "By the time I got home…"

"You forgot," Donna finished. "Well, then, this will be a pleasant surprise."

"What will be?"

Donna grinned but said nothing.

The restaurant smelled of spicy French fries and charcoal-broiled burgers. Merry's mouth watered, but she cringed when she saw the long line of people waiting for tables. Every booth and every one of the many four-top tables scattered throughout the expansive dining room were occupied. The bar was crowded, too, with multiple TVs tuned to the college basketball game. Periodic yells or boos erupted from fans, depending on which team made their shot.

Merry glanced around at all the twentysomething women with drinks in hand. Many wore reindeer ears or strings of blinking Christmas lights, while handsome young men sporting tacky Christmas ties flirted with them. Her ugly holiday sweater didn't seem so out of place after all. "Donna, we don't have reservations. We'll never get a table."

Donna winked, crooked her finger, and headed off toward the back of the restaurant.

Merry groaned but followed. Through a set of open French doors, she saw a semi-private dining room and finally realized what that missed text must have been about. A group of her work colleagues were glued to a TV, sipping beers, and diving into accessible plates of hors d'oeuvres sitting atop the shoved-together tables. "Donna Ferguson, I thought you said it was just the two of us. You dragged me half an hour away on a school night to get together with coworkers I can see up in Belford tomorrow?"

"It's not a school night," Donna shot back. "And yes, I had to use a little subterfuge to get you out to socialize. I'm actually relieved you didn't read that text." She turned and waved at Stefanie Summers, the art department chair, who was engrossed in the basketball game while guzzling a large mug of beer. Donna pulled up two chairs from a nearby empty table and sat, indicating Merry should take the other seat.

Stefanie raised her glass in greeting. "Hey, Mrs. Halliday, glad you could make it."

Merry hated when the twentysomething called her "Mrs.," making her feel like the woman's teacher rather than her colleague. Stefanie was only a second-year art teacher in Donna's department, and yet she had just been named Department Chair, leapfrogging over more experienced teachers, Donna in particular. At age sixty-two, Donna had shrugged it off, but she and Merry both knew that educators at their experience and pay level were considered an expense that strained the school's budget. And Thomas Belford Prep had a very tight budget.

Merry just hoped to complete her last few years of teaching with her pension and dignity intact, rather than be prematurely forced out by the school board.

She shook off those dark thoughts and decided that, since she was here and hungry, she might as well enjoy the evening. Donna was right; she didn't go out much anymore. She smiled at Stefanie Summers, hoping she had a designated driver after downing that tankard of beer. Merry nodded to long-time chemistry teacher George Johnson and stopped herself from giggling when she observed special needs teacher, Katie Harris, openly flirting with Matteo Muniz, the young history substitute teacher.

Soon-to-be retired head football coach Ralph Barrows waved from across the table, while holding hands with his bride of forty years.

Merry waved back to them. "Good to see you, Ralph, Barb."

"You a basketball fan?" Coach asked Merry.

"Are you?" Merry shot back.

Coach grinned and took a swig of beer. "The Oklahoma football team won't make another appearance until bowl time New Year's Day, so we displaced Sooners have to console ourselves with whatever's available."

Merry glanced up at the TV screen. Second half, Indiana University sixty-eight, Oklahoma sixty-two. She started to comment on the Sooner's score deficit when her stomach growled again, so she asked no one in particular, "Do we have a server?"

Stefanie shook her head and waved her arms around to indicate the crowded restaurant. "You'll have to go to the bar and order something, Mrs. Halliday."

"Thank you, Miss Summers." Merry meant that as a subtle dig.

The young woman just giggled and took another swallow of beer.

Merry turned to Donna. "Can I get you anything?"

Donna nodded, her gaze fixed on the TV. "Light beer and nachos. Whoohoo! Go Hoosiers!"

It was after eight p.m. Motivated by hunger and thirst, Merry elbowed her way to the crowded bar in the center of the restaurant, causing some of the younger patrons to give her the side-eye.

A young man slid off his barstool to go flirt with a pretty woman who walked by, so she plopped down as fast as she could. *Now to get the bartender's attention.* She drummed her fingers on the wooden bar as she attempted to make eye contact. Then she saw the bartender's nametag, Kelli T, and recognized her as the mother of her student Kristina. Merry briefly wondered why Mrs. Timmons was tending bar at a restaurant a half hour south of Belford, when she worked all day as a realtor's administrative assistant. But Merry knew the answer. Mrs. Timmons was the sole breadwinner of their large family.

Merry leaned across the bar and waved. "Hellooo! Mrs. Timmons. Kelli?"

"Good luck with that," said someone behind her.

Merry turned to see a handsome man with thick salt-and-pepper hair, wearing an expensive silk business suit that seemed out of place for a night of beer and basketball. "Have we met?" Merry asked.

His blue eyes twinkled with laugh lines that deepened as he smiled. "I'm Gr…uh." He hesitated a moment before extending his hand to shake. "Name's Keith. You are…?"

"Merry." She shook his hand and wondered why such an attractive man would be flirting. If that's what he was doing. And she wasn't really sure, because it had been nearly thirty-five years since she'd dated any man.

"Hi, Merry. Can I buy you a drink?"

"I'm with some work friends," she said, tilting her head in the direction of the back room, "but apparently we're on our own if we want anything to eat or drink."

Keith winked. "Here. Let me give it a try." He caught the bartender's eye and smiled at her as he pulled out an Amex card. "My friend here would like to place an order."

Merry didn't want this guy thinking he could buy her a drink, but she also didn't want to miss the opportunity he'd created. "Hi, Kelli. Remember me? Kristina's English teacher?"

Kelli blushed, smoothed her apron and smiled. "Sure. How can I help you?"

"Bottle of light draft, a diet cola, and a large order of nachos. Loaded." She thrust her arm in front of Keith's to present her own credit card to Kelli. "We're in the back room over there. Can someone…?"

"We'll bring it to you." Kelli ran the credit card and set about pouring the drinks.

Merry slipped the receipt in her pocket and smiled at Keith. "Thanks for your help." She slid off the barstool and headed back to join Donna and their coworkers.

But Keith didn't take the hint, instead following right behind her. Fending off bar flirts was way out of her comfort zone, but maybe Donna would know what to do. After all, she'd been divorced and in the dating scene for years. Arriving at their table, Merry gave Donna "the look."

Apparently Donna ignored "the look," because she smiled at the man and gave him a not-too-subtle onceover. "Who's this?"

"Keith," Merry replied through gritted teeth. "He helped me get the bartender's attention." She gave up hoping he'd go away when he pulled up a chair and sat down between her and Donna. *Maybe he's interested in Donna.* Even though Donna was a couple of years older than Merry, she was attractive and always dressed stylishly to accentuate her full figure.

"I'm Donna Ferguson." She waved at her colleagues. "All of us are teachers, out to celebrate the end of the semester."

There were a few mumbled greetings, but most everyone was engrossed in the game, which now included Keith. He shouted, "Go Sooners!" when the visiting team scored a three-pointer.

Coach Barrows reached around his wife and offered the newcomer a high-five.

Donna lifted an eyebrow. "You don't live around here, do you?"

Keith blushed. "Nope. Just in town for business. Guess I should root for the local team, huh?"

"What sort of business brings you to Indianapolis?" Merry asked.

"Actually, not Indianapolis. I have business up in

Belford, a small town just north of here. Plus I have a son who lives here, so it's sort of a combined business and pleasure trip."

Donna winked at Merry and said to Keith, "We're familiar with Belford."

Merry was about to ask what sort of business he had in such a small town, when a server appeared with their drinks and food.

"Thank goodness." Donna took a large swallow of her beer.

Merry reached for her soda, but she didn't want to be rude to their…guest, party crasher? She wasn't sure, so she pointed to the nachos. "Care for some?"

"Oh, that's very kind, but I have to call it a night. Go ahead and enjoy your evening." Keith stood, turned his back on Donna, and gave Merry a warm smile. "It was nice meeting you, Merry. Maybe we can get together again while I'm in town." He slipped her his business card and left.

As she stuffed it in her jeans pocket and dug into the cheesy nachos, Merry didn't give another thought to the business card.

Chapter Two
Thursday, December 20

Merry reached over, hit snooze on her five-thirty a.m. alarm, and nearly drifted back to sleep.

That is, until Spookie jumped up onto the bed. "Meow."

"You're right." She stroked the cat's silky fur. "Time to get the day started." She threw her legs over the side of the bed and stepped into the house slippers she kept nearby to avoid the cold, hard floor. She still hadn't gotten used to the fact her bedroom lacked carpet, unlike the home she'd lived in with Bert. Maybe she should invest in an area rug? That might be the perfect compromise, sort of a bridge between her old life and the new one she was creating for herself.

No students would be at school today, since their final exams were over and vacation started yesterday, so she could dress casually. Coffee mug in hand, Merry surveyed her closet. Eyeing the overflowing laundry hamper, she decided the jeans and Christmas sweater she'd worn the night before were perfectly fine. She had no one to impress. Besides, her colleagues at school would be dressed in festive holiday wear, too, all while enjoying the annual cookie exchange after their faculty Christmas luncheon.

Cookies! Merry reached into the kitchen cupboard where she'd stored a fresh batch of her homemade sugar cookies, the ones she baked in abundance every year. They were not only tasty but a family tradition.

Growing up, the Bell family didn't have a lot of extra money, so every Christmas, Merry's grandmother gave her and her cousins homemade sugar cookies in festive holiday shapes, all baked with love. While they were still warm, Grandma topped the bells, trees, angels, stars, and snowmen with green and red sugar sprinkles, which seemed to melt into the gooey softness. And since Merry's birthday was the day after Christmas, Grandma always snuck her a few more cookies than her cousins.

Once she was old enough to help her grandmother in the kitchen, Merry loved learning to make the dough, chill it in the fridge for a couple of hours, and then roll it out. Her favorite part was using her grandmother's old-fashioned, metal cookie cutters to form the Christmas shapes. After Grandma passed away, Merry inherited the cookie cutters and became the official family baker at the age of sixteen.

She stuffed the plastic container full of cookies into her briefcase, glanced around for Spookie, but didn't see her as she left for work.

The school always seemed so empty and cavernous when the kids weren't there. Merry entered the building from the faculty parking lot and walked through the entryway foyer, with its larger-than-life, nineteenth century painting of Thomas Belford, the town's founder. Her footsteps echoed down the long hallway, the heels of her boots hitting the concrete flooring as she made her way to her classroom, now cleared of yesterday's party debris.

The big old building, that had in better times

housed over two thousand students, now had an enrollment of less than four hundred. The district lines had been redrawn, and most of the student population had moved across town to the newer and larger Belford High School, with its state-of-the-art computers, new athletic facilities, and giant performing arts center.

Stately but showing its age, Thomas Belford Preparatory High School desperately needed school board approval for costly repairs if it hoped to remain open. Merry and her fellow teachers all knew some sort of reckoning was coming, but no one was willing to speculate on what that might be. Still, there were plenty of whispered conversations in the faculty lounge and furtive glances cast at strangers who entered the building.

"Good morning, teachers and staff!" Principal Alexander's voice boomed over the Public Address system and echoed down the empty hall. "We have a busy day planned. There's our holiday luncheon at noon, followed by our annual cookie-baking contest, a guest speaker at our afternoon faculty meeting, and of course, your grades must be submitted online by four o'clock. But until then, I hope this puts you in the proper mood." "Jingle Bells" blasted through the speakers.

Thankfully, Dr. Alexander turned the volume down moments later. In her classroom, Merry was just booting up her computer when Donna appeared in the doorway.

"Merry Halliday," she said, hands on hips. "Are you wearing...?"

Merry felt her cheeks redden. "Yes, the same jeans and sweater I had on last night. Don't judge. I haven't had time to do laundry." She dug into her briefcase, pulled out a stack of still-ungraded student essays, and waved them at Donna. "If there are no other insults, I'll see you at lunch."

Donna harrumphed and flounced out, the giant bells fastened to her shoelaces jangling as she went.

Fifty essays graded, three losing games of computer solitaire, and a head start on January lesson plans later, Merry heard a light tap on her open door. Expecting to see Donna back for round two, she turned instead to see one of her students standing in the doorway. "Kristina Timmons?" Merry eyes widened as she motioned her in. "Oh, my goodness, what happened to you?"

Kristina lifted her right arm, now in a sling. "Volleyball game last night. I was going for the winning shot when I collided with one of my teammates and hit the floor." She groaned. "Mrs. Halliday, I need that volleyball scholarship to get into college."

"And I'm sure you'll get it," Merry hastened to say. She walked a bit closer to visually survey Kristina's injured arm. "What did the doctor say?"

Kristina blushed and looked down at her feet. "The team trainer said there might be a wrist fracture."

But your mother doesn't have any insurance. Merry sighed. "Does it hurt?"

Kristina shrugged. "I'll be okay. I came in to check on my final essay. I couldn't wait till grades come out. If I can't play volleyball, I can at least maintain my four-point grade average."

Merry frowned. "Kristina, it's way too soon to give up on your athletic scholarship." She thumbed through the graded papers on her desk until she located Kristina's and smiled as she handed her the paper. "*A plus.* I couldn't find anything to criticize, hard as I tried. Excellent analysis of the symbolism of the three spirits in *A Christmas Carol*."

Kristina beamed as she looked over her paper. "Can I take this?"

Merry nodded.

Kristina, with her left hand, carefully placed the essay in her handbag. "Thanks, Mrs. Halliday. And Merry Christmas."

"Same to you, and your family." Merry allowed herself a moment of worry. Kristina would be the first in her family to attend college, assuming she didn't lose her scholarship. Which she might, if Kelli couldn't find a way to get Kristina's wrist treated by a doctor. Soon.

"Staff," Dr. Alexander said, coming back on the PA, "our PTA-prepared luncheon is served in the cafeteria. And don't forget about our guest speaker this afternoon."

The savory aromas of roasted turkey and pumpkin pie spice wafted down the hallway, causing Merry's stomach to growl. She couldn't help but wonder if Belford Prep was about to be served up on a platter, as well.

****

Discussion during the luncheon turned to the identity of the mysterious guest speaker.

Coach Barrows tucked his Santa-themed Christmas tie into his shirt as it threatened to fall into the gravy. "Maybe someone's making a donation for my cash-strapped athletic program?"

Stefanie Summers gave Coach the side-eye. "No

way," she said, as she adjusted her green pointy elf hat. "Everyone loves visual arts, and I heard an anonymous donor is planning to sponsor an art show at the mall featuring our students. So if there's any extra money, we're getting it. Don't you agree, Ms. Ferguson?"

Donna swallowed her bite of turkey and glanced at Merry. "I really wouldn't know." She pushed back from the table, empty plate in hand. "Excuse me. I'm going back for seconds."

"Bring me a biscuit?" Merry understood Donna's need to avoid confrontation with the new art department chair.

George Johnson sniffed. "My science room desperately needs updating. Belford High across town just got a state-of-the-art chemistry lab, at taxpayer expense I might add."

Matteo Muni, the young history sub, yanked off his stocking cap and shook out his dark brown ponytail. "Although I'm just subbing till Mrs. Hayward gets back from maternity leave, even I know the history textbooks are old and outdated." He turned to see Katie Harris smiling at him and winked at her.

Katie blushed. "Well, yes, but what about new manipulatives and art supplies for the Special Needs classroom?"

"No," Merry said with a flourish of her fork. "Any of those one-time cash infusions would be great, but they won't fix our long-term problems. I have a feeling our guest is the school superintendent here to talk about consolidating with Belford High." She sighed.

After the meal, the faculty trickled into the library for the meeting, each with a sampling of the various cookies baked by their colleagues. Merry noted with pride that every single plate contained at least one of her decorated sugar cookies.

Donna eased herself into a wooden chair next to Merry and stretched her legs under the table. "After that meal, I'm more in the mood for a nap than a staff meeting." She patted her belly. "But it's a good thing I saved room for the cookies. Yours are amazing."

Dr. Alexander, dressed as usual in a business suit, stepped to the podium that faced the study tables where the teachers had gathered, and tapped the live microphone. "Is this thing on?"

"We hear ya, Doc," Ralph Barrows called from the back of the room.

"Wonderful," she said into the mic, which squelched. She took a step back. "First, I'd like to thank our dedicated PTA moms for the holiday meal they prepared."

Everyone applauded.

"And I'd like to announce the winner of this year's annual cookie baking contest." She glanced around the room and beamed. "For the third straight year, our winner is Merry Halliday!"

Merry rose to applause from her colleagues, went to the podium to accept the ten-dollar gift certificate to her favorite coffee shop, and returned to her seat.

"And now we have to get down to business," Dr. Alexander said. "As you know, Thomas Belford Preparatory High School has seen a decline in enrollment over the last few years. We've had to tighten our belts and cut corners in order to afford things like electricity, books, and teacher salaries. Structural repairs have been put off way too long. The school board has been discussing ways to alleviate the financial burden on the taxpayers, and they've come up with what we all agree is a viable solution."

Merry sat straight in her chair, every muscle fiber on high alert. "Here it comes," she whispered to Donna.

"The solution to our problems," the principal said, "is to convert to a charter school."

Merry gasped and glanced around at her colleagues, who all seemed as stunned as she did. Turning their beloved small-town school into a corporate-run business was her worst nightmare.

"So, ladies and gentlemen," Dr. Alexander said with a rap of a pen on the podium, "I'd like to introduce our guest speaker. This gentleman has come all the way from South Bend, Indiana, the corporate headquarters of Lake City Prep Academy, to explain the transition. Please welcome Gradison Williams." Dr. Alexander clapped as if she were introducing a celebrity.

Gradison Williams emerged from the librarian's office as if he were a rock star, smiling and waving both hands at the staff as an eerie silence descended on the room.

Merry's jaw dropped.

"Merry?" Coach Barrows tapped her shoulder. "Didn't we meet…?"

"Isn't that…" Donna whispered.

Merry held up a finger. She dug into the pocket of her jeans and fished out the slightly crumpled business card from the man who called himself Keith. She hadn't even bothered to look at it before, but now she put on her glasses and studied it carefully.

Gradison K. Williams, Attorney at Law/Consultant
Lake City Prep Academy, South Bend, Indiana
Responsible Educational Directives

25

Donna glanced at the business card. "Yep, I'm seeing RED all right."

Merry sputtered and then stifled a giggle.

"Thanks, everyone," Mr. Williams said into the mic. "I know you have questions about charter schools in general, and Lake City Prep in particular. So I've prepared a PowerPoint to give you an idea of how we can improve Thomas Belford High's academic standing, make needed repairs to the building, and jump-start the arts and athletic programs."

At that, both Coach Barrows and Stefanie Summers let out a whoop.

"I can see how eager you are, so let's get to it, shall we?" He nodded to Dr. Alexander, who lowered the lights.

Merry seethed as Keith, or Gradison, or whatever he called himself, flashed pie charts, bar graphs, and Venn diagrams on the screen. Every one of them was designed to prove what a superior service they offered, based on the success of their schools in the Chicago area. But tiny Belford wasn't Chicago, and she didn't think their tactics would work in small town Indiana.

"Raising test scores," Gradison told them, "is our number one priority. Any questions?"

Merry raised her hand. "Mr. Williams?"

Gradison surveyed the room until he saw Merry.

He appeared as startled to see her as she'd been to find him standing in her school's library.

"Um, hello there. Pleasure to see you again. Question?"

"Yes." Merry stood and glared. "Those test scores. How many students were tested?"

"Um, I believe the school tested about one hundred

pupils."

"And do those test results include special needs students?"

"Well, uh, no," he stammered. "I don't believe, that is we don't actually have the ability to…"

She went right on. "And did all the students who began the school year take those exams at the end of the year?"

"Um, I'd have to check on that."

"So then no," Merry concluded. "And the teachers? How many have Masters of Education degrees? Are they paid accordingly?"

Gradison looked down at his shoes. "Well, many of our teachers hold degrees in their subject matter, but…"

"Many?" Merry was incredulous.

"You mentioned athletics." Ralph Barrows stood, his jaw clenched and his eyebrow lifted. "But I don't see football anywhere on those charts."

"Or volleyball," Merry added. "Belford Prep has a top-rated team."

"As you can see," Gradison said, turning his back to point to the screen, "we offer our students an opportunity to participate in competitive sports such as track and basketball."

Instead of returning to his seat, Coach Barrows leaned against a bookshelf, his arms crossed as he glared at Mr. Williams.

Katie Harris, who doubled as the volleyball coach, stood and mirrored his stance.

"How long is the school year, Mr. Williams?" Merry asked.

He ran his fingers through his thick, salt-and-pepper hair. "Our school year is about twenty days longer than the public school calendar, and we require our students to go to tutoring sessions either after school or on Saturdays."

"But many of our students have to work," she said. "I don't see how…"

Gradison held up a hand. "My staff has put together packets of information about our program, our policies and procedures, our staffing needs, and pay scales. We'd like you to go over the information during the school break." Without making eye contact—with Merry or anyone else—Gradison reached behind the podium, extracted a large file box, and began distributing the packets.

Donna opened her envelope, thumbed through it, and pulled out a page, waving it in the air. "I see that teacher salaries will be lower than we now earn, benefits reduced, and yet, we'll be expected to work more days and longer hours. How can we be required…?"

"Ladies and gentlemen, we can table this discussion until after the winter break." Dr. Alexander tapped the microphone to regain control of the meeting. "The school board and I agree these changes are necessary if we want to keep the school open."

"Well, I'm excited!" Stefanie Summers jumped to her feet. "I think this is a great opportunity. When do we start?"

Gradison smiled and seemed to relax a bit. "January. As soon as you return from holiday break. Students will get one extra vacation day, so we can train teachers on our online grading system and the required lesson plan format. So have a great holiday and come back ready to dig in."

Chair legs scraped the linoleum floor. Teachers grumbled on their way out of the library as Dr. Alexander shook Mr. Williams' hand and took her leave.

He turned his back on the exiting faculty to pack up his laptop.

Merry approached the podium and cleared her throat. "Hello, *Keith.*"

He turned around, blinked, and surveyed her outfit.

Merry glared. Even though Keith, or Gradison, was a handsome man, she was too angry to feel self-conscious about her recycled attire.

But he was the one who appeared uncomfortable. "Um, well, this is…was…I mean, last night when I mentioned Belford…"

"Why did you tell me your name is Keith?"

He blanched. "I used to go by Keith back in college, and sometimes…"

"…You use it when hitting on women in bars," Merry finished for him.

He took a deep breath and offered his hand to shake. "Please, call me Grady. I'm sorry we got off to a bad start, but I meant it when I said I'd like to see you again."

Merry gave his outstretched hand a perfunctory shake, turned on her heel, and fled.

Yes, Belford Prep needed an infusion of cash, and their students' standardized test scores had been low the last few years. Still, Merry didn't believe a single test was a good indicator of her students' abilities, yet Dr. Alexander had brought in someone specifically to raise those test scores. What would a new focus on testing mean for her career?

****

Merry flung open her classroom door and slumped into her desk chair. She swallowed hard and stared up at the stained ceiling tiles. *Now what?* Being fired or forced into early retirement was a distinct possibility, especially after how rude she'd just been to Mr. Williams. She gazed around her classroom. On the walls were clichéd motivational posters: *Believe and Succeed. Learn Something New Today. Dream Big.* Hanging in the back of the room was a bulletin board crammed with students' writing assignments and notes from kids offering encouragement to each other. She loved that about her students—when a kid didn't get a top grade, classmates wouldn't let them give up on themselves.

Where would that camaraderie go when the charter school pitted one child against another as they clawed their way to the top of the test scores? And where would her creative lesson plans fit in? Her annual Charles Dickens Day, with kids reading aloud from his works with accompanying art work from Donna's classes, would be thrown out in favor of test prep.

She gazed at the depleted bookshelf under the window. Many of the novels and biographies, books she'd provided at her own expense, had either vanished, been damaged, or were hopelessly outdated. Merry had tried to rearrange the remaining books to disguise the empty shelves, since the school couldn't purchase any more nonessential items. *Books, nonessential.* She laughed at the irony, but it was indicative of the financial predicament the school was in. Merry currently had only twenty copies of *A Christmas Carol*, not nearly enough for a classroom of thirty or more students, so this year she allowed her students to access online versions.

"You forgot this." Donna walked into the classroom waving the manila packet in the air.

"If only I could forget," Merry said. She resumed her slump.

Donna tossed the packet on Merry's desk. "I'm sure we'll be wowed by Lake City's innovative teaching style."

She chuckled at Donna's sarcasm. "Careful, they're soon to be our bosses."

Donna rolled her eyes. "If I don't get forced into early retirement."

Merry shuddered. "I was just thinking the same thing." Her master's degree and years of experience earned her higher pay. And Mr. Williams' comment that *many* teachers had advanced degrees seemed to indicate the charter school didn't value them. She took a deep breath. "When do you leave for Houston?"

"You're changing the subject."

Merry shook her head. "There's no sorting this out till after the holidays, so I want you to have a good time with your family."

"It takes a half hour from my house in Melville just to get to Belford, and then over an hour from here to the Indianapolis airport, so I'm leaving in the wee hours of Christmas Eve morning," Donna said. "My granddaughter is flying down when she gets done with her college finals, so hopefully we get some girl time while I'm there."

Merry started to withdraw her lesson plan book from the top desk drawer, but working on second semester lessons now seemed moot. She reached for the packet and perused its exterior. "Do you think Lake City Prep will tell me—us—what to teach, when, and how long to spend on each element of the lesson?"

"Probably." Donna sat on the edge of Merry's desk. "But maybe it'll be easier that way. Just let the bosses do our thinking for us."

Merry lifted an eyebrow. "And stifle our students' creativity and imagination." She tossed the manila envelope into a desk drawer and slammed it shut.

Donna reached across the desk and gave Merry a quick hug. "You spending Christmas with Robin?"

Merry slumped her shoulders as she remembered the text she'd gotten from Robin a couple of weeks ago. She pulled her phone out of her handbag, scrolled through the texts, and handed it to Donna.

—Eli and I are taking a pre-honeymoon trip starting Christmas Eve through New Year's, since we'll both be too busy at work to take any time off after the wedding in June. We're going to Hawaii! Details later. XOXOX—

Donna's eyes bugged out. "Your only child and her boy toy…"

"He's twenty-eight."

Donna went right on, "…are leaving you alone on both Christmas and Boxing Day?" She returned Merry's phone.

Donna's mention of her upcoming sixtieth birthday made her cringe. "I'm sure Robin and Eli will call, or video chat or something."

Donna clucked her tongue. "Merry, I…"

She waved away whatever admonishment Donna was about to offer. "Shoo. Go home. Don't you have a date tonight? That banker?"

Donna stood and headed to the door. "Date number three. What about you?"

"Dinner with Robin, Eli, and Eli's father." Merry groaned inwardly as she gathered her belongings.

"Didn't Robin say he's single, and cute?"

Merry held up a hand. "Don't even think about mentioning a fix-up."

Chapter Three
Thursday, December 20

"Spookie?" Merry called as she walked in her front door after work. She dropped her coat and briefcase on the sofa and went to the kitchen to open a can of cat food, but she thought it odd Spookie hadn't eaten any of her food from this morning. Merry rinsed out the dish and refilled it but still no Spookie. Now she was worried. She recalled not seeing her before she left for school. Had the cat gotten out somehow?

She checked all the cat's usual hiding places. The built-in desk in the kitchen she used as an office? Not there. Under her bed? Nope. Not in the back of the bedroom closet nor snuggled under the sofa cushions in the living room. Not behind the washer or dryer. Not anywhere in the bathroom. Alarmed, she called out again. "Spookie?"

Merry heard a faint "meow." She followed the increasingly urgent cries to the coat closet near the front door, opened it wide, and there sat her black cat atop a pile of Christmas decorations. "Oh, poor kitty. You spent the whole day in there?" Merry clicked her tongue as Spookie darted out of the closet, ran to the kitchen, and dove into her food dish. "I'm so sorry, Spookie. From now on I promise to look before I shut any doors."

She surveyed the closet, hoping a bored, trapped

cat hadn't caused any damage. But perusing the closet reminded her that all her holiday decorations were still packed away in there, rather than festooning her condo. The first year after Bert's unexpected heart attack and sudden death, Merry tried to follow their established tradition and put up a tree in the large family home, but her heart wasn't in it. Bert always insisted on a live tree, but she realized getting the tree home and wrestling it into the tree stand was more than she could handle. So that year she didn't have a tree at all.

In better spirits the next year, she purchased a smaller, artificial tree and hung as many of the family keepsake ornaments as it would hold. The treetop silver star from years past looked at home there.

Merry surveyed her small living room, completely devoid of holiday spirit. Part of her had to admit she'd put off decorating because no one would be here to see it. Still, she could decorate for her own enjoyment, so she set to work.

She took the small, pre-lit tabletop tree from its box in the coat closet, set it on the end table, retrieved the boxes of ornaments stored in the back of her bedroom closet, and in short order, her condo looked quite festive. It was amazing how a small artificial tree and a couple of stockings dangling from the key rack by the door, one labeled Merry Carol and the other one Spookie, could lift her mood.

Her phone rang. She scooped it off the coffee table with a quick glance at the caller ID. "Hi, Robin."

"Mom? Hi, I'm kind of in a rush right now. One last meeting with the new client before I can leave work."

Merry did an exaggerated eye roll, once again glad

they weren't on video. "I understand you're busy, Robin, but you called me, so…"

"I'm calling about dinner tonight. Don't forget Eli's dad is in town. We're eager for the two of you to get to know each other."

"I haven't forgotten." Merry resisted the urge to groan at Robin's transparent motives, but she figured she'd have to meet Elijah's parents at some point.

She knew very little about them. Eli grew up in South Bend, Indiana, near Chicago, went to college and law school at Notre Dame University, accepted a job with a firm in Indianapolis, and then met Robin, whose marketing firm had mutual clients with Eli's law firm.

Merry knew Eli's parents divorced when he was in elementary school. His mother lived somewhere near downtown Indianapolis with her husband, and Eli's dad lived and worked in South Bend.

"So, dinner?" Robin asked.

"As long as this is just a meet and greet and not a fix-up."

"Sure, okay. Paddy's Bistro on Broad Ripple Avenue, eight p.m." Robin disconnected.

Merry would have preferred to change into her comfy sweats, snuggle with her cat, and watch a holiday movie by the light of her just-decorated Christmas tree. Instead she showered, dressed, and drove a half hour into Indianapolis to meet Elijah's father.

****

Paddy's Bistro was a popular hangout for young professionals. Many came straight from work in their business attire, unlike the uber-casual sports bar from last night. Merry had to let her eyes adjust to the mood-setting dim lighting before wending her way to the hostess stand, which was a bit removed from the main entrance. The restaurant had no four-top tables, only brown, high-back wooden booths, and they were filled with thirtysomethings sipping wine and nibbling on tiny platters of gourmet hors d'oeuvres.

"Hi, Mom." Robin appeared at her mother's side, gave her cheek a quick peck, pulled back, and looked Merry up and down. "You look nice."

"You don't have to sound so surprised." Merry glanced down at the gray, V-neck sweater she'd paired with a pair of black dress trousers. "I want to make a good first impression on your fiancé's dad, and it's not what you're thinking."

Robin was dressed in her usual business casual—skinny designer jeans, navy blazer over a crepe blouse shoved to the elbows, and high heels. Very high heels. Aside from the fact that wearing jeans with heels had been a no-no when Merry was her daughter's age, she couldn't imagine how Robin managed to walk in those things all day.

Merry stood on tiptoes to see over the tops of the booths. "Where's Eli?"

"He's picking up his dad at his hotel downtown. They should be here soon."

"Halliday, party of four," the hostess called.

"Here!" Robin waved and stepped to the hostess stand. "My fiancé and his father will be joining us. Can you show them to our booth?"

Merry and Robin followed the hostess to the back of the expansive restaurant. Their booth in the middle of an aisle, but with the high backs, it still felt private.

The hostess set four menus on the table. "Can I get you ladies anything to drink?"

"Two glasses of chardonnay." Robin held up a hand to stop her mother's objection. "Relax, Mom. You're on vacation."

"But I do have to drive home." Merry slipped on her glasses and perused the menu. The smell of meat and shrimp sizzling on a grill whetted her appetite.

The server returned with their chardonnays.

Merry took a small sip, decided it was too dry, and set aside the glass.

Robin peeked over the top of her menu. "I'm glad you came tonight, Mom, and I'm so excited you're going to finally meet…"

"There you are." Eli leaned down and kissed Robin's forehead, gave Merry's shoulder a squeeze, and scooted into the booth next to his fiancée as he indicated the man next to him. "Merry Halliday, I'd like you to meet my father, Gra…"

"Gradison Williams?" Merry was thunderstruck. This was the third time in two days! First as a party crasher, then the face of the charter school, and now Eli's dad?

She metaphorically slapped her forehead. How could she not know, not put the pieces together? Elijah Williams from South Bend, Indiana. Gradison K. Williams, also from South Bend. Williams was a common last name, true, but now she berated herself for not seeing the resemblance between the two men. They were both about six feet tall, lean and muscular, with deep blue eyes, and Gradison's salt-and-pepper hair must have originally been dark brown like his son's. Merry shook her head in disbelief. "Keith and I have met."

Robin and Eli exchanged surprised glances.

"My friends call me Grady." He blushed, hesitated a moment, and then pointed to the seat next to Merry. "May I?"

Merry lifted an eyebrow but scooted over.

Eli leaned his elbows on the table. "Dad, no one calls you Keith except that old fraternity brother of yours. And Mom."

Grady blushed and picked up a menu.

Robin shifted her gaze back and forth between her mother and her fiancé's father. "What do you mean you two have met?"

"Last night," Grady told her. "At a sports bar not far from here. Your mother was with some of her work colleagues." He fiddled with his napkin and silverware.

"And again today." Merry returned to perusing the menu.

Robin lifted a quizzical eyebrow as she took a sip of wine.

For her part, Merry couldn't believe the man who was about to upend her career was also about to become family. In a way. She thought about excusing herself to the ladies' room and then walking straight to the parking lot, but she didn't want to embarrass her daughter. So she decided to go ahead with this farce of a dinner.

"So, Merry," Eli said, "I think I told you my dad's an attorney." He glanced at Robin, who nodded. "But he's been working as a consultant for a charter school company, and he's in town in that capacity."

"Do tell." Merry flipped a page in the menu but didn't look up.

Grady took a deep breath. "The charter school, Eli," he said, "is acquiring Thomas Belford Preparatory High School, as of January third."

Robin nearly spit out her wine. "Acquiring?" She grabbed her glass of water and took several swallows.

Merry set the menu on the table and patted her daughter's hand. "Taking it over, dear. I'll soon be put out to pasture."

"No," Grady exclaimed. "I mean…that's not what…"

Merry turned her attention to Grady and blinked. "I apologize, Mr. Williams. I'm sure Lake City Prep is very professional when it lays off teachers."

"Mom," Robin hissed.

Merry sighed and crossed her hands in her lap. "How long must…will you be staying in Indianapolis?"

Grady took a few breaths and a couple of slow sips of water. "After today's presentation, I had planned to leave town tomorrow, but Eli convinced me to stay a few more days. Holidays and all."

"How nice."

Grady shot a pleading look at his son.

"So, Dad, you and Robin's mom will be working together?" Eli glanced back at Grady and shrugged, as if that was the best he could do.

Grady cleared his throat and nodded. "I had no idea the woman I met last night was your mother, Robin, and that she and her friends were all teachers at Thomas Belford Prep. But if you ask me," he said with a smile at Merry, "it was fortuitous."

She remembered her first impression from last night—that he was handsome and sophisticated. Part of her wished she could go back twenty-four hours and relive her ignorant bliss. But now that she knew who he was and the company he represented, it rankled.

He shoved aside his menu. "Since we're about to become in-laws, I'd like the chance to start over. If that's okay." He offered his hand to shake.

For her daughter's sake, Merry couldn't refuse to shake his hand, nor could she ignore his attractive smile. "Yes, I suppose a do-over is in order."

Robin visibly relaxed. "I knew you two would hit it off."

"And I look forward to meeting Eli's mother as well." Merry hoped that would put a stop to her daughter's attempts at matchmaking.

The server took their orders and collected the menus.

Merry endured dirty looks from her daughter as she refused to contribute anything to the conversation, staring at her phone as if she expected a message to come through at any time. Finally their food arrived.

Grady pushed his French fries around the plate with a fork, while Merry picked at her grilled chicken salad, not taking more than a couple of bites.

Robin and Eli chatted about their work day, traded bites of their salmon and steak dinners, and tried to engage Merry and Grady in conversation. The weather. How delicious the food was. The busy holiday season. None of those generic topics went anywhere.

Finally, Merry had had enough, signaled the server, and requested a take-home box.

Robin's eyes widened. "You're leaving?"

"I have to be up early tomorrow." She filled the square paper box with the remainder of her salad and snapped shut the lid.

"Why? School's out," Robin said.

"The Good Samaritan food and toy drive. We meet in the gym tomorrow to organize the donations and get them ready to go to the recipients. And I'm bringing my cookies for the refreshment table, so I've got to get baking."

"Were those your Christmas-shaped sugar cookies at the luncheon?" Grady asked. "Because I ate a couple, and they were amazing. Light and fluffy, and you use real vanilla, not imitation, right?"

Merry smiled in spite of herself. "Yes, thank you."

"See?" Robin said, glancing between them. "You already have something in common. Great-grandma's sugar cookies."

Grady pushed aside his half-eaten burger and glanced over at Merry. "Good Samaritan. Sounds like a worthy cause."

Merry bit her tongue. *What would you know about worthy causes?* "It is." She gathered her coat, handbag, and food box.

"Do you need any help?" Grady asked as he let her out of the booth. "With the charity drive, I mean?"

Merry ignored him. "It's been great seeing you kids." She blew a kiss to Robin and placed some cash in front of Eli for what she assumed was her share of the dinner tab, plus a reasonable tip.

"Mom," Robin said with a groan. She gave Eli a look.

"Dinner's on us." Eli returned the bills to Merry.

"If you insist." She stuffed the money into her purse. "Call me, Robin."

Once at the restaurant's front door, she had a moment of guilt, realizing she probably hurt her daughter's feelings by leaving so abruptly. She juggled her handbag and carryout food box, trying to figure out how to get into her coat, when Grady came up behind her and helped her into it.

"I'm sorry we got off to such a bad start. Is there anything I can do to fix this?"

Merry turned to face him. "Get your company to back off?"

He blinked.

"No? Well then…"

"I meant it when I offered to help with your charity drive," Grady said. "I have an SUV available to help."

Merry's emotions about Gradison Williams and his sudden appearance in her life were all over the place. She reached for the door. "Have a good evening, Mr. Williams."

"Please call me Grady," he called after her.

Chapter Four
Friday, December 21

Merry had told Robin that little white lie last night to give herself an excuse to leave that awkward dinner. She would be at school to help out with the charity food and toy drive like she did every year, but not as early as she'd let on. Her contribution was the refreshment table, including about six dozen of her popular sugar cookies. She planned to bake her cookies and arrive about noon, after a long soak in a warm bubble bath.

She had just run the bathwater when her phone rang. Realizing she left it on the living room coffee table last night, she wrapped herself in a towel, stepped into her slippers, and scurried out of the bathroom, answering the phone just before the call went to voice mail.

"Oh, Mom, I was just about to leave a message. Did I interrupt something?"

"I was about to step into the tub." Merry walked over to the oven and set it to preheat.

"Oh, sorry. Well, you rushed out so fast last night that Eli and I didn't get to give you the details of our upcoming trip."

"Details?"

"Yes," Robin said, "our pre-honeymoon. Remember?"

If only I could forget. But she didn't want to make

her only child feel guilty for enjoying her own life, and Merry did still remember what it was like to be young and in love. "I'm eager to hear all about it."

"We got our plane tickets and hotel reservations for the twenty-fourth. We're going to spend Christmas in Hawaii. *Mele Kalikimaka*," Robin exclaimed.

Merry swallowed hard. She thought—hoped, even—that their holiday vacation would be more like a weekend in Chicago. Instead they were going a couple of time zones away. She forced herself to sound cheerful. "Sounds lovely."

"I know you usually spend time with your friend Donna over the holidays. Will she be celebrating your birthday with you?"

She nearly blurted out Donna's travel plans but bit her tongue. After all, a sixtieth birthday wasn't so special that she wanted to deprive her daughter and soon-to-be son-in-law of this romantic trip. "Don't you worry about me," Merry said. "You and Eli go and have a wonderful pre-honeymoon." She disconnected the phone just as the preheated oven beeped.

Time to lose herself in cookie baking and forget about her bleak Christmas holiday plans.

****

Merry checked the institution clock on the school gymnasium wall. It was just before noon, which allowed plenty of time to set up the refreshment table before the volunteers took a break, and the families came to collect their donation boxes. She brought several cases of bottled water, had pre-arranged for cheese platters from the school's cafeteria, and, of course, had dozens of her still-warm cookies to set out.

PTA moms, a couple of dads, and a few teachers

had taken over the entire gym floor, bustling about filling boxes labeled for each of the hundred or so families who requested help from Good Samaritan. The gym's bleachers had been shoved against the walls and the basketball goals moved out of the way to make room for piles of new, unwrapped toys, clothing, and huge barrels of nonperishable food items.

Merry always enjoyed helping out with the Christmas charity, and she understood the need, as she'd watched the surrounding neighborhoods decline over the last several years. A local factory that manufactured heating units moved its operations to Mexico and laid off workers. Many more jobs disappeared when a large department store went out of business. And then three elementary schools consolidated into one, costing many of the teachers their jobs.

She glanced at the busy workers and shook her head at the small number of volunteers who showed up, knowing they'd need more help. The student members of the school's Service Club had spent the week collecting all the donations from various bins around town and transporting them to the gym, but their part was done. It was the holidays and people had plans, so the few dedicated adults who were here had a herculean task ahead.

Merry shivered and tied her sweater a little tighter around her waist. She noticed volunteers working with their coats and gloves on in the chilly gym, since the school always turned down the heat during school breaks to save on the exorbitant electric bill.

She spotted the lunchroom table for the refreshments, already set up in the corner under the scoreboard. Slinging her large, reusable shopping bag—containing her cookies, napkins, and paper plates—over her shoulder, she strode purposefully across the hardwood floor.

"Yoohoo! Merry!" Donna sprinted across the gym floor. "I thought you'd abandoned us." She leaned her hands on her knees to catch her breath.

"You know I'd never bail on this event." Merry lowered the heavy bag from her shoulder and set it on the table. "I brought the cookies and bottled water. The cheese and cracker trays I ordered from the cafeteria should be ready to pick up."

"I'll go get them while you set up here." Donna took off in the direction of the school cafeteria.

In the meantime, Merry dug into her bag and pulled out the Christmas-themed paper tablecloth she'd bought at the dollar store, the bulk package of napkins and plates that matched them, and finally, her six dozen, freshly-baked cookies. A hint of vanilla wafted out as she opened one of the plastic storage boxes. The holiday shapes added color and festivity to the table.

The bottles of water were still in her car. She was about to go back out to retrieve them, when Donna rolled in a cart containing two restaurant-sized platters of cheese and crackers.

Together they placed the platters between plates of cookies--leaving space for the water--and made sure everyone could easily access napkins and paper plates. Merry dragged over a trash bin so it was within easy reach, then stood back and admired her handiwork. "What do you think?"

"Yum." Donna grinned as she reached for a cookie and took a bite.

Merry smiled at her friend. "I need to go get the bottles of water from my car. Can I borrow that cart?"

"Need help?" said a voice behind her.

Grateful for another volunteer, Merry smiled as she turned, and then gulped. "Grady! What…?"

"I told you I wanted to help."

Merry felt a bit off-balance as she gazed into those deep blue eyes, but shook it off and almost sent him packing. That is, until she remembered how short-handed they were. "Since you offered, you can get the cases of bottled water in the trunk of my car. It's the blue, mid-sized sedan parked near the gym's entrance." She handed him her key fob and indicated the now-empty cart.

Grady commandeered the cart. "On it." He was outside and back in moments, and he had the cases of bottled water unloaded onto the refreshment table in record time. When he returned Merry's key fob, she pooh-poohed the thought that she'd felt a tingle down her spine when their fingers touched.

"What else?"

"We're short of volunteers over there," Donna said with a wink and a head tilt.

Merry rolled her eyes at Donna's flirting, but Grady didn't seem to notice as he went to pitch in with the other volunteers.

A couple of hours later, families began streaming into the gym—children wide-eyed, their parents looking haggard—to retrieve their holiday boxes filled with non-perishable food, clothing for each member of the family, and toys for the children. Merry encouraged volunteers and families to help themselves to snacks and cookies.

She watched Grady from afar, not knowing what to think. Last night she hadn't believed his offer of help was sincere, yet here he was. Still, Merry wondered if he could truly see the need in the community. After all, he was a wealthy, professional man, come to wreak havoc on a school with cash-strapped families and teachers who needed their paychecks.

The afternoon passed quickly as the gym emptied of most of the filled charity boxes. The last of the cookies disappeared as families made their way out.

Donna appeared at Merry's side, coat on, ready to leave.

"Whose boxes are those still in the corner?"

Donna furrowed her brow. "The Timmons family. Apparently Kelli couldn't get off work, and no one else in the family drives."

"What? No!" Merry couldn't bear the thought of her favorite student going without for the holidays. "What do we do?"

"I've got another date with the banker tonight, so I can't stay. And the gym's going to be locked for the next two weeks in..."—Donna glanced up at the gymnasium clock—"less than an hour. Can you stay in case she shows up?"

"I don't mind waiting, but Kelli Timmons probably won't make it here in time. What a disaster." Merry crossed her arms, patted her foot, and thought for a moment. "Okay, since I know the family, I'll deliver the boxes myself."

Donna raised an eyebrow as she glanced at the six very large boxes set aside for the Timmons family. "How?"

Merry slid into her coat. "You go and enjoy your

evening. I have an idea how to fix this."

Donna shrugged and waved goodbye.

Fingers figuratively crossed, Merry hurried across the gym and approached Coach Barrows, who was shaking hands with Gradison Williams. "Excuse me Ralph. I need to borrow Grady."

He turned. "Borrow me?"

Merry always believed that old cliché about a person catching more flies with honey than vinegar. She motioned him aside. "Thank you so much for all your help today, but I need one more favor."

He smiled, a warm and engaging smile that lit up his entire face. "Like you said, it's a worthy cause. And I enjoyed getting to know some of Belford Prep's faculty and PTA parents. So what can I do for you?"

Merry berated herself for thinking poorly of Grady. After all, he'd been helping out all day when a number of scheduled volunteers never showed up. She felt a twinge of guilt for harboring doubts about his character, and she actually liked his smile. "I'm a bit concerned. The custodian is locking the building in..."—she glanced up at the clock—"...well, soon, and I just found out the Timmons family never picked up their charity donations."

"Who?" Grady asked.

"Kristina Timmons, one of my students. She's also a talented athlete, but she recently got hurt in a volleyball game and probably has a broken arm."

Grady frowned. "That's a shame. Did she see a doctor?"

Merry shook her head. "No health insurance. And an athletic scholarship is the only way Kristina can go to college."

He scratched his head. "Unfortunate, but what's that got to do with the Christmas donations?"

"It means Kristina's family is struggling, and her mom needs these items or there won't be a Christmas."

He nodded. "What can I do to help?"

"Mrs. Timmons works two jobs, one of them at that sports bar where we met the other night, and she's probably already at work. I'd deliver these boxes to the Timmons home myself, but they won't all fit into my small sedan. I know you have an SUV and…"

Grady followed her gaze to the boxes stacked against the wall. "Shall we?" He set about stacking one large box on top of another and headed to the door. "Can you carry any of those?"

Merry tested a couple of boxes and found one she could lift. Grady's SUV was parked near her sedan, and by the time she lugged her box outside, she saw he was already shifting shopping bags around inside to make room.

"Shopping for Robin and Eli," Grady explained without being asked.

Merry craned her neck to see what he'd been shopping for, but all she could see was a large box of lasagna sticking out of the top of one bag.

"That looks heavy." Grady took the box from her and set it inside the vehicle. "How many more?"

"Three."

Between the two of them, they got the last three boxes out of the gym as the custodian jangled his keys, tapped his foot, and stared at the clock.

His SUV held all but one, which he squeezed into Merry's trunk. "Should I follow you to the Timmons house?" Grady asked. "We'll probably have to unload the boxes if your student's arm is broken."

"Right." Merry leaned against her car door to catch her breath as she thought about the Timmons' family's predicament. "I'm hoping Kristina's arm gets treated by a doctor soon, and the worst that happens is she has to switch high schools in January."

Grady blinked. "Why would she switch high schools?"

Was he really that clueless? She stood and turned to face him. "Although Kristina's an honor student, thanks to your charter school, no athletics means no athletic scholarship. She'd need to transfer to another school for the softball season. Assuming her arm heals in time."

"I thought she was a volleyball player."

"She's both," Merry said, "and quite good."

Grady was quiet for a moment, then he nodded. "I get it, but…"

"Do you?" Merry swiped a finger through her hair, realizing she could use a cut and color.

"Maybe not, but I'm hoping you can help me understand." Grady opened his car door but turned back before getting in. "Didn't you wonder why I was food shopping? After all, I'm staying in a hotel."

"I have to admit it crossed my mind."

"I'm headed to Eli and Robin's townhouse to make dinner tonight."

Merry's jaw dropped. "You cook?"

He nodded as he took out his phone and fired off a text. "Single men who want to eat have to cook." The phone pinged with a response, he read it, and then wiggled the phone in front of Merry. "I asked Eli if I could bring a plus one. What do you say? Are you brave enough to try my cooking?"

Merry thought about it. If she went home she'd be eating leftovers, so what was the harm in having a home-cooked meal at her daughter's house? And why did she feel like she'd just been asked on a date? "The Timmons' house is about a mile away." She got into her car, started the engine, checked the rearview mirror, and rolled down the window. "And yes, I'll join you and the kids for dinner."

Emphasis on *the kids*, Merry told herself.

****

"Mom?" Robin gaped.

Merry hugged her daughter and whispered, "Don't read anything into this."

Eli blinked. "When you said you were bringing a plus one to dinner, Dad, I thought…"

Grady carried his grocery bags into the kitchen. "Merry and I had an interesting afternoon." He winked at Merry.

"Together?" Robin and Eli asked at the same time and with furtively exchanged glances.

Merry took off her coat and hung it in the entry hall coat closet. "Grady helped me make a last-minute Good Samaritan delivery," Merry told Robin before turning to Eli. "And your father said he was planning to cook dinner for you two. It was kind of him to include me, and kind of both of you to allow me to crash your dinner party."

After another awkward pause and more surprised glances between Robin and her fiancé, Robin jumped into hostess mode. "Can I offer you a drink, Mom?" She crossed the room to the built-in wet bar in the formal dining room.

Merry remembered Robin's excitement when she purchased this ultra-modern, newly-built townhouse. Robin raved about the front entryway that offered a view of the entire downstairs and its expansive, open-concept kitchen, and she hired a designer for the living room, resulting in magazine-worthy, contemporary decor. The stainless-steel kitchen appliances, hardwood floors, and monochromatic paint colors all reflected the esthetic Robin loved. Once she and Eli became engaged, he gave notice at his apartment and moved in.

Merry could hear Christmas music playing in their upstairs loft, or study, or home office, or whatever they were calling it. She crossed the room to get a closer look at the Christmas tree—a six-foot, artificial tree with tiny, twinkling white lights—sitting in front of the large picture window. She reached out to touch a few of the ornaments from Robin's childhood.

Robin put an arm around her mom and handed her a glass of white wine. "Thanks for saving those for me."

The two of them sat on the sofa and chatted while Eli worked on his laptop at a white, wooden, built-in corner desk.

An hour later, divine smells emanated from the kitchen.

"Anybody hungry?" Grady called from the kitchen.

Merry's stomach growled as the aroma of tomatoey lasagna, laced with garlic and oregano, wafted from the kitchen. "Need any help?" She went into the kitchen fully intending to be of service but blinked at the sight.

Grady had used multiple pots and pans, and the mess was visible from every corner of the downstairs, reminding Merry why she hated these modern, open-concept living spaces. Her first instinct was to start cleaning up, but she remembered how Bert felt about her "help" on the rare occasions when he was the chef. He always came up with a delicious meal, but he left the kitchen a wreck.

Grady followed her gaze and blushed. "I know it looks bad, but I've got a system."

Merry decided it wasn't her place to criticize, and the food did smell delicious. "Far be it for me to stifle creativity." She called to the living room. "Robin? Need help setting the table?"

Robin, who was staring intently at her phone, waved her hand in the direction of the kitchen. "Feel free, Mom."

She had to get the plates and silverware out of the kitchen cabinet, which meant averting her gaze from the mess as she skirted around the center island. Merry made her way to the cabinet where Robin kept the dishes and retrieved four plates and four salad bowls. She started to set them down on the marble counter while she pulled eating utensils out of the nearby drawer, but accidentally backed into Grady, who was removing the lasagna from the oven. "Oh, sorry, I…"

"Oops, hot dish," Grady said at the same time.

They both giggled nervously, and Merry stepped back. "Man with the hot dish has the right of way." She waited till he put the bubbling casserole on top of the stove before she scooted past him with the dinnerware. "Just one more minute and I'll be out of your way." She retrieved eating utensils and then opened and closed several drawers in search of placemats and napkins.

"Looking for something?" Grady gave the salad a final, professional-appearing toss.

Merry was impressed with his culinary skills, if not his housekeeping. "Placemats." She scouted out the chaotic kitchen. "Robin's very protective of her dining room table."

"I think I saw them over there." He tilted his head toward a cabinet where Robin kept the drinking glasses.

Merry shifted the silverware to her other hand and opened the cabinet. Inside were wine glasses, coffee mugs, cookbooks, extra paper products, plastic storage containers, and near the back of the top shelf, placemats and napkins. "I see them, but…"

"Here, let me." Grady set aside the salad tongs and reached around her into the cabinet.

She felt her cheeks redden as he brushed against her. "Thanks," she mumbled.

After setting the table, Merry felt very warm. Without her glasses, she squinted at the hall thermostat, which she thought read sixty-seven degrees. Just as she was about to go find her glasses and check again, she cooled down. *Maybe it was being in the kitchen close to the hot oven.* Of course. That had to be it.

"Dinner is served." Grady placed the casserole dish on a trivet in the middle of the table and set the salad next to it.

Robin dimmed the lights and lit a couple of candles, creating a warm, romantic feel. "Before we sit down, I want everyone to join hands. Like we used to do when Dad was alive." Robin reached for Eli on her right and took Merry's hand with her left.

Eli clasped his father's hand.

There was an awkward pause before Grady gingerly took Merry's hand.

"In keeping with the season," Robin said with a

wink at her mom, "which was very special to both my parents, I'd like to give thanks for the meal we're about to eat and for bringing us all together tonight."

Merry squeezed Robin's hand before releasing it. "Your father would have loved seeing you so happy."

They pulled out their chairs, chitchatting about how good the food looked, how hungry they were, and the fast-approaching holiday.

As they tucked into their meal, which was as delicious as it looked and smelled, Merry marveled at how her life and association with Gradison Williams had radically changed in the space of a few days.

And how her association with him could change her future.

Chapter Five
Saturday, December 22

Since all her sugar cookies were eaten at the Good Samaritan event, Merry spent the morning baking more. She then braved a trip to the grocery store filled with last-minute holiday shoppers, which required a good deal of time and patience.

Exhausted, she stepped into her condo with her bag of groceries and called for Spookie. She heard the cat rustling around in the bedroom, so she set the bag on the kitchen counter and went down the hall to see what mischief the cat had gotten into this time.

"Spookie, what in the world?" Merry shook her head. The cat was perched atop a pile of her jeans and sweatshirts, clothes that had been in the overflowing laundry hamper she'd been ignoring for days. Spookie must have overturned it, dragged everything out onto the floor, and then made a nest for herself. Before Merry could pick up the mess, the doorbell rang. "Behave," she told the cat on her way to the front door.

She peeked through the peep hole, smiled, and flung open the door. "Paul. Come in." He was one half of the young couple who moved in next door a few weeks ago. Merry liked them both immediately. Paul Satterfield always smiled and waved or stopped to chat at the mailbox, acting more like he was welcoming Merry to the neighborhood than the other way around.

Making a new friend felt good.

Paul held up a platter of something that smelled of cinnamon and ginger. "Merry Christmas." He pulled aside the foil covering to reveal still-warm gingerbread, cut into bite sized squares.

Merry reached for a square and moaned with pleasure as she took a bite, warm crumbs falling on her chin. She motioned him into the kitchen, grabbed a tea towel, and wiped the crumbs. "That's obscene," she said around a mouthful of bite number two.

Paul set the plate on the kitchen counter. "My husband does all the cooking, but baking is my thing."

Merry nodded and swallowed. "You're an amazing pastry chef. Peterson's Coffee Emporium is lucky to have you." She pulled a plate of her own Christmas sugar cookies from the pantry and handed it to Paul. "I was going to deliver these today, but since you're here…"

Paul rubbed his hands together before biting into a sugar cookie shaped like a Christmas tree. He grinned. "You're no slouch yourself. How do you even have time to bake?" He finished off the cookie and reached for another.

"That's high praise coming from a professional baker." Merry blushed with pleasure. "I start before Thanksgiving. I make about six batches of dough, freeze them individually, and thaw as needed. Each batch makes about sixty cookies. Can I offer you some tea? Coffee?"

Paul shook his head. "I've got to get home. Just making my Christmas delivery."

"Well, thanks for the goodies. I really needed the pick-me-up after the morning I had. Shopping the last

Saturday before Christmas is a nightmare, and then Spookie…" Merry shook her head, at a loss for words.

"What did that adorable kitty do?"

Merry crooked her finger and led Paul in to see the disaster on her bedroom floor.

"She's sending you a message." He lifted an eyebrow at the mess and gave her current attire, yet another pair of mom jeans and a Belford Prep sweatshirt, an obvious once-over. "Time for a new wardrobe."

Merry opened her mouth to object but realized she had no defense. Robin had been nagging her to get rid of her mom jeans, and those sweatshirts had seen better days. Even Donna had waggled her finger, claiming nobody wore sweatshirts anymore except maybe for gardening, and Merry didn't have a garden.

She sighed. "I know. But I'm terrible at picking out fashion. If you don't believe me," she said with a wink, "ask my daughter."

Paul grinned. "Girlfriend, you're in luck. Today's my day off, everything is marked down for the holidays, and I'd be happy to be your Queer Eye for fashion." He checked the time on his phone. "Meet me at the mall in two hours."

Merry showed Paul to the front door. "It's a date."

****

Nowadays most of Merry's friends, in fact most people in general, preferred to shop online and avoid the holiday crowds, but Merry had always loved the mall at Christmas time. Even today, as crowded as it was, she still enjoyed browsing and people-watching. She'd already ordered most of her gifts online and had them gift wrapped and delivered, but the red, green and silver decorations, mixed with scents of gingerbread and cotton candy, gave the bustling shopping center a nostalgic appeal.

The mall's main artery was adorned with green and red lights, interwoven with garlands that crisscrossed the exposed overhead rafters. A large Christmas tree stood in the center of the walkway, hovering over a tiny Santa's hut that was festooned with fake snow and more twinkling lights. A long line of parents and kids snaked around the hut and well down the mall. Moms shifted babies in their arms while wiggly toddlers whined, laughed, or clung to their mother's legs or arms. Young women, some no more than teenagers, in short green skirts with jaunty red caps, escorted eager, cranky, or frightened children one at a time to see Santa. The big guy himself sat on a painted gold throne with a red velvet seat and laughed jovially.

The piped-in, generic Christmas music was designed to get shoppers in the mood to open their pocketbooks, and judging by all the people carrying shopping bags, it was working. Merry hummed along with the familiar tune as she perused the various department stores and smaller specialty shops, each elaborately decorated, and each store with a sign advertising a sale. *50% OFF! BUY ONE GET ONE! TODAY ONLY!* That was misleading, of course, because the sales would continue till the mall closed Christmas Eve and begin again first thing on December twenty-sixth. The day the British and Canadians called Boxing Day.

She groaned inwardly, knowing her sixtieth birthday was mere days away. *Now where was I supposed to meet Paul?*

He texted an hour ago. He insisted the big anchor department store would be too crowded and the merchandise too picked over. Instead he knew of a small, out-of-the-way boutique where they had what Paul claimed was the most amazing couture and instructed her to meet him at two o'clock.

Couture? Merry knew that was code for out of her price range. A quick glance at her wristwatch, the one Robin said she didn't need any more since she could check the time on her phone, told her she was late. She spotted a mall directory, quickly perused it, found The Style Shop, and took off at a brisk pace to the opposite end of the mall. Unfortunately the number of slow walkers, moms pushing strollers, and window-shoppers impeded her progress, causing her to fret Paul would give up on her.

Out of breath, she eventually arrived in front of what was indeed a small shop, tucked off in a corridor that Merry never frequented. In fact, the only other things down there were a hair salon and vending machines, and the soda dispenser's flashing light read *Out of Order.* She wondered how the clothing store stayed in business, suspecting it was from over-priced merchandise. She opened The Style Shop's glass front door, decorated with black, swirly lettering, and stepped inside.

"Yoohoo, Merry!" Paul waved from a back corner of the tiny shop.

He'd changed clothes from this morning, looking handsome and stylish in skinny jeans, a navy polo-type sweater over a collared shirt, and thick, black-rimmed eye glasses. Merry crossed the store to join him. "Sorry I'm late." A young woman, very young in fact, making

Merry think she could have been one of her students not too long ago, joined the two of them.

Paul gave Merry a quick shoulder squeeze. "This is Peri, short for Periwinkle. She goes to the local community college by day and is a server in the evenings at the Peterson's Coffee Emporium where I work. And in between that, she finds time to work in this delightful, little boutique."

Peri stuck out her hand to shake. "I'm a fashion major, so based on how little they pay me, it's really more like an internship."

Merry clasped her hand and glanced around the shop, oddly devoid of shoppers considering how crowded the mall was. An aisle down the middle of the store separated the junior clothing from the women's sizes. On the junior side were jeans, colorful tops and sweaters, leggings, and dresses that could be worn for an occasion such as a holiday party or Prom. On the women's side, the selection was more conservative—career outfits like trousers, suits, skirts, and blouses.

When she caught sight of a price tag on a size twelve blouse that read one hundred forty dollars, she gulped. And that was the marked-down price. She began thinking of excuses to extricate herself from what could end up being a budget-busting shopping spree. "These selections are lovely, but…"

Peri laughed. "Didn't Paul tell you?" She led Merry and Paul to a corner rack at the back of the store. "We're phasing out some of our women's career selections, marked them way down, and I've pulled some things that I'm sure will fit your new look."

"My new look?" Merry lifted an eyebrow at Paul. "You know I'm a widow *and* a school teacher, right?

Neither of those things scream fashionista or big spender."

Paul patted her arm. "I told you to trust me."

Peri ran her finger along the sales rack until she came to the size eights and waved a hand at them. "Ta dah."

Merry thumbed through the selections, if for no other reason than politeness. She admired the quality of the clothing but winced at the price tags.

Peri pulled a handful of items off the rack and headed in the direction of the fitting rooms.

Merry reluctantly followed. *Maybe I'll get some good fashion ideas and then go to the department store and use my coupons to buy something similar on sale.*

"I want you to come out and model everything that fits," Paul told her.

The store's front door opened. "I'll be right with you, ladies," Peri called to two teenage girls who wandered in.

Peri handed Merry a stack of clothes to try on, some on hangers and some folded. "Some of the jeans run small so I also brought some size tens just in case. Let me know if you need anything." She closed the dressing room door.

Merry glanced at her mirror reflection. A few more lines had appeared around her eyes and mouth, and her formerly auburn hair was now dry and lackluster, with flecks of gray at the temples. She wondered if a wardrobe update was enough to offset the fact she was officially old.

She chose a pair of the jeans, a style much tighter than she ever wore, but once she was in them, found them comfortable and flattering to her tall, slender figure. She then chose a lovely burgundy blouse with a black open cardigan and stepped out of the dressing room.

Paul whistled and gave her two thumbs-up.

"I have to admit these are nice," Merry said, "but…" She held her breath as she glanced at the price tag but was pleasantly surprised. The two-hundred-dollar jeans had been marked down several times and were now priced at fifty-nine dollars, an amount her budget could handle. The blouse and cardigan were equally discounted. "Really?"

Peri crossed her arms, stood back, and looked Merry up and down. Finally, she gave the outfit an approving nod. "The truth is, we mostly cater to teens and twentysomethings these days, and the women's styles just don't sell."

"See? I told you I knew where to shop." Paul rocked back on his heels and beamed.

In the end, Merry bought three pair of jeans, four blouses, one khaki-green choker-neck sweater and one black turtleneck sweater, the black cardigan plus a burgundy one, a pair of gray trousers, and the navy blazer—all for just a few hundred dollars. Giddy, she shifted the store bags to one hand and reached to give Paul a hug with the other. "I can't thank you enough."

"You're welcome, but we're not done yet." He pointed to the beauty salon adjacent to the boutique. "Time to liven up your 'do'." He waved goodbye to Peri, took Merry by the hand, and led her into the salon. He waved at an attractive young man with pink hair and diamond stud earrings and turned to leave. "Next time I see you, Merry Halliday, you'll be a new woman." Paul sailed out of the salon.

She was left behind with the hairdresser, who was already running his fingers through her dry, lifeless hair.

"Might as well get comfortable," he said. "We've got a lot of work to do."

Chapter Six
Sunday, December 23

Merry had no reason to get up at nine-fifteen on Sunday morning, but she was wide awake. She closed her eyes and attempted to drift back to sleep but finally gave up, stretched, and tossed off the covers. Almost immediately she pulled them back when she saw her breath form condensation in her bedroom. She snuggled back beneath the blankets until she felt brave enough to slide out of bed and grab her bathrobe. The vinyl floor felt like ice under her feet as she stepped into her house slippers.

She shivered as she went into the hall to check the thermostat. "Fifty-four?" Was the furnace broken? Where would she get a repairman on the Sunday before Christmas? And how much would the overtime charges be? She'd been told when she closed on the condo that the HVAC system was over ten years old. *Maybe the system will hold out till January.* Assuming she still had a job in January. She sighed and cranked up the heat, crossing her fingers that it kicked on.

Spookie rubbed against her leg. Merry reached down to scratch her behind the ears and stepped into the kitchen to open a can of cat food. *Hot coffee!* She reached for the coffee pot but on a whim, picked up her phone and punched in Donna's phone number. After several rings it went to voicemail.

"Hi, Donna, just wondering if you wanted to go to brunch. I'll catch you another time."

Well, it was freezing in this condo, so with or without Donna, Merry was going out to breakfast. She ran the shower extra hot until it steamed up the bathroom, the warm water splashing over her as she lathered up. Clutching her robe around her on the way to the bedroom, she passed the hall thermostat, which now read sixty. Fingers crossed.

She studied her reflection in the bedroom mirror and smoothed down a lock of hair. The stylist had cut her hair in the chin-length bob she preferred and added a richer shade of auburn, which had the added benefit of covering the gray. She liked the new look.

Now, what to wear? She had no one to impress, but those lovely new clothes in her closet were beckoning. She chose skinny jeans and a black crepe blouse, turning this way and that to get the full effect in the mirror.

****

"Table for…?" the server asked as Merry walked into the Sun Up Café.

"Just me." Merry's stomach rumbled as she inhaled the mingled aromas of freshly brewed coffee and cinnamon rolls. The small, popular breakfast restaurant, located in a strip mall near her condo, was nearly full on this cold December morning, making Merry feel guilty for needing a table for one. The server made a big show of pulling one menu off the stand and leading her to a table meant for two in the back of the restaurant, next to the kitchen. A quick glance around the busy restaurant told her she was lucky to get a table at all.

He set the menu in front of her. "Coffee?"

"Please." Merry opened the menu, even though she ate here often and practically had it memorized. She wished she'd stopped to pick up a copy of the Sunday newspaper, but without anything else to read, she took her time perusing her breakfast choices.

"Mind if I join you?"

Merry looked up from her menu and blinked. "Grady?"

He didn't wait for an invitation but smiled as he sat down across from her. "Good morning."

Merry's heart thumped wildly in her chest, and her stomach lurched. Was that butterflies or hunger? She couldn't tell. "What are you doing here?"

Grady shrugged and picked up Merry's menu. "Breakfast."

"No, I mean what are you doing *here*? At this restaurant."

Grady set down the menu and leaned his arms on the table. "A guy gets tired of the continental breakfast fare at the hotel. Robin suggested this place. She said it's your favorite. Great pastries and…"

Just then the server arrived with a carafe of coffee and one mug.

"And gourmet coffee." He made eye contact with the server. "If you don't mind."

The server nodded and soon returned with a second coffee mug.

Merry studied Grady's face, curious why he would drive all the way up to Belford for breakfast, Robin's recommendation notwithstanding. Had he hoped to run into her, or was he just bored with the hotel fare like he said? She didn't know him well enough to figure that out.

Watching Grady pour them both coffee and lift his mug in a mock toast, she could have sworn his eyes twinkled. *Stop it, Merry. You're not a lovesick schoolgirl*. He was her daughter's future father-in-law, and worse, he was the man about to upend her career.

But then Merry thought back to the dinner Grady cooked two nights ago and the warm, family atmosphere he helped create at Robin's. She let go of her righteous indignation, for the moment anyway, and smiled. "I'll have to remember to thank my daughter."

The server returned, tablet in hand. "You folks know what you want?"

"Separate checks." Merry produced the gift card she'd won at the school cookie baking contest and scooted it across the table to the server. "Cheese omelet, hash browns, and one of your fresh-baked cinnamon rolls."

Grady handed over the menu. "I'll have the same, except add an order of bacon." He reached for the sweetener carousel and proceeded to empty three packets and pour a generous serving of creamer into his coffee.

Merry lifted an eyebrow at Grady's excess as she swallowed her black coffee. But she miscalculated how hot it was. She set down the mug too hard, causing the coffee to slosh out, waved her hand in front of her face, and then took a large gulp of cold water. When her tongue finally cooled off, she noticed Grady smirking.

He took his napkin and wiped up some of the coffee off the table and waved over the server, who offered yet another roll of his eyes as he finished wiping up the spill.

Merry was mortified. "I'm sorry. I…"

"Don't worry. Accidents happen." Grady reached across the table, squeezed her hand, and smiled. "I'm just glad we have some time to get to know each other better."

Merry hesitated a moment before withdrawing her hand. "You seem like a nice man. But just to be clear, I hate the idea of a corporate takeover of any public school, and you work for the one that's commandeering mine."

He winked. "Duly noted."

She managed a smile. "But we do have Robin and Eli."

Grady smiled back. "If you ask me, that's a lot."

The server arrived with a tray of food and set their dishes in front of them.

Merry tucked in, acutely aware that she was sharing a meal with a very handsome man.

****

Donna arrived on Merry's doorstep mid-afternoon, gift bag in hand.

"Sorry I missed your call this morning. I slept in." She stopped and gave Merry a once-over. "Wow, you look amazing! What brought all this on?" She pointed at Merry's attire and new hairdo.

Merry motioned her inside. "My next-door neighbor, Paul Satterfield."

Donna lifted an eyebrow. "Your neighbor just came over and announced you needed a makeover?"

"It was a little more involved than that," she said. "Paul stopped by with some tasty baked goods right after Spookie got up to some mischief, and I returned the favor with some of my own cookies. And I don't mind saying, Paul the pastry chef was impressed."

"I've always said those cookies of yours could open new doors." Donna assessed Merry's new outfit from every angle. "Your neighbor did you a favor. It was time…"

Merry put up her hands in surrender. "Time to retire the mom jeans. I know. I've got a bag of items ready to donate to Good Samaritan." She led Donna into the kitchen, poured water from the whistling tea kettle into two cups, and offered Donna a choice of tea bags from the tea caddy. "Cookie?"

"Of course." Donna dunked a tea bag into the boiling water, reached for a cookie, and glanced up at Merry. "This is my official dropping-off-my-gift visit. I have an early flight to Houston tomorrow morning, and I didn't think you'd want a visitor at four a.m." Donna blew on the hot tea before taking a sip and set it aside as she held out a small Christmas gift bag. "It's a combination Christmas and birthday gift, despite the wrapping."

"Shall I open it?"

Donna shrugged.

So Merry opened the bag, removed the tissue, and withdrew a box containing a Christmas ornament. "First Christmas in the new home." She glanced up. "That's so thoughtful."

"I know this is technically your second Christmas here, but the company doesn't make those."

"It's still a lovely gesture." Merry carefully took the ornament out of the box, walked around the tabletop tree till she located an available spot, and attached the ornament. "There. Perfect." She beamed at Donna.

"My work here is done." Donna took a couple

more sips of her now-cooled tea and set down the cup.

"I already sent your gift to your son's house, but..." Merry opened a cabinet and withdrew a plastic bag containing a half dozen of her sugar cookies. "For the plane, to go with the complimentary airlines coffee."

"Yum. Thanks! I'll call you from Houston." Donna glanced around Merry's living room as she opened the front door. "I hope you don't sit here in this nicely decorated condo all by yourself over the holidays." She waggled a finger. "I mean it." She hugged Merry on her way out.

Merry didn't know how to tell Donna she *was* spending the holidays alone, so she plastered on a brave smile, waved goodbye, and shut the door.

Chapter Seven
Monday, December 24

The jazz station Merry loved blasted Christmas music into the bedroom, Sinatra crooning one of her favorites. Jarred awake, she realized her alarm was still set for a school day. She shut it off and almost drifted back to sleep, until Spookie jumped on her pillow, meowing and head-bumping.

Merry stroked the cat's head, tentatively stuck a toe out from under the covers, decided the room felt fine, and climbed out of bed. Her HVAC was working again, for the moment anyway. She pulled on her bathrobe, went into the kitchen, and flipped on the coffee pot as Spookie paced back and forth in front of her empty dish. Once it was filled, Spookie dove in while Merry poured her coffee.

Ding-dong ding-dong. Bang bang bang. "Mom?" *Bang bang bang.* "Mom? Are you up?"

Startled, Merry set her coffee on the kitchen counter. "Robin?" She tightened her bathrobe as she padded to the front door. "For heaven's sake, what are you doing here at this hour?"

Robin and Eli stood on the front porch holding hands, grinning and jumping up and down to keep warm.

Small wonder, since both were dressed in shorts, tennis shoes, and only a sweatshirt against the early morning cold. "Is something wrong?" Merry waved them in.

Robin gave Merry a bear hug. "No, nothing's wrong. We just wanted to wish you Merry Christmas and an early happy birthday."

Merry lifted an eyebrow. "At seven o'clock in the morning?"

"We're off to Hawaii for our pre-honeymoon. Remember?" Robin reached into her oversized handbag and withdrew two gifts—one wrapped in glossy red holiday paper and artfully tied with a green bow, the other in pink and white Happy Birthday paper.

"I remembered your flight was today, but I didn't know what time."

Eli grinned. "Our flight leaves Indianapolis at ten, and then we've got a four-hour layover in Denver. But with the five-hour time difference between Denver and Honolulu, we still get to Hawaii by late afternoon. Plenty of beach time." He reached out and squeezed Robin's hand as they exchanged excited glances.

"But it *is* Christmas Eve," Robin said, "and we didn't want to leave town without giving you your gifts."

Pleased that her daughter hadn't completely forgotten her, Merry still felt sad that this would be the first Christmas and birthday they had ever spent apart. Realistically, with Robin soon-to-be married, there might be many more separate holidays. She sat on the sofa and slowly removed the Christmas wrapping from the small box, lifted the lid, and then gasped. "You bought it!"

Robin sat on the sofa next to her. "Of course I did."

Last summer, Merry and Robin were browsing in

an out-of-the-way antique store in Donna's hometown of Melville, Indiana. Merry oo-ed and ah-ed over a turn-of-the twentieth century silver locket, dangling on a thick chain. "I always wanted a locket, and this one is beautiful. But it was so expensive." She glanced up, puzzled. "How did you…?"

Robin grinned. "As soon as we left the store, I texted the owner and asked her to hold it for me. It was a little extravagant, but I wanted you to have it. Look inside."

Merry gently opened the locket to discover a tiny picture of Robin and Eli smiling back. The photo must have originally been a selfie, but they'd gone to the trouble of having it printed and sized to fit the locket. "Thank you." Merry beamed. "Both of you."

Robin helped her mother fasten the clasp around her neck. "And now the birthday gift."

Merry reached for the other bag and withdrew a department store jewelry box. Inside, she found a pair of silver dangly earrings with a vintage design. She held them up to her ears. "How do I look?"

"Awesome!" Robin winked. "They flatter your new 'do."

Merry blushed, happy that her daughter had noticed her new look, and approved.

"I know the earrings are new," Robin said, "but I thought they complemented the locket."

Merry stepped into the bathroom and admired the locket in the mirror, turning this way and that to get the full effect. It really was a lovely piece. The earrings were perfect with it, just as Robin said. "Wait, I have something for you." Merry headed to the kitchen.

"We already got the gifts you ordered us online,

Mom."

"Something else." Merry opened her pantry, pulled out the cookie tin covered in Christmas decals, and set it on the counter. She retrieved a large plastic bag from a lower kitchen cabinet, filled it with a dozen of her special sugar cookies, and zipped it closed. "Just a reminder of home."

Robin's eyes lit up. "We'll get some coffee at the airport and have these for breakfast." She took the cookies and kissed her mom on the cheek.

Merry gathered her courage. "You two had better be off now. Can't have you missing your flight."

Eli reached for the doorknob. "Got any plans for the holidays, Merry?"

Merry had no intention of inflicting a guilt trip on her obviously over-the-moon daughter and her fiancé, so she smiled and made an effort to sound breezy. "Oh, the guys next door have asked me over." It was a little white lie, but who knew? Maybe they would. Or something else could come up. If not, there were worse things than a little alone time. "You two have a wonderful vacation. Text me some beach photos." She held the door for Robin and Eli and watched them get into their car.

Merry waved goodbye as they drove away. She slumped against the closed front door and fingered her locket. Bert was gone, Robin had her own life, and now, she needed to get on with hers.

If only she could figure out how.

****

"Now what, Spookie?" The holiday film ended, and Merry turned off the TV.

"Meow." Spookie jumped onto the sofa, circled

Merry's lap, and curled into a ball, purring.

It had been a few hours since Robin and Eli's impromptu visit, but all she'd managed to accomplish was to change from pajamas into sweat pants and a well-worn hoodie sweatshirt.

This week had been a whirlwind. Baking her special cookies for family and friends was exhilarating, since everyone raved about them. She got to help her favorite charity, including a family she cared about, but that very family and so many others in her school were about to be overrun by a corporation whose attorney was soon to be part of her family. It was enough to make her head spin.

Now she faced three days alone, with plenty of time to agonize about it all.

Her phone rang, jolting her out of her pity party. She set Spookie on the floor. "Hello? Donna?"

"Merry Christmas, Merry Carol Bell Halliday!"

Merry smiled. Every holiday season Donna liked to use her full name, the name her parents had given her to commemorate her holiday birth. "How's Houston?"

"Surprisingly warm," Donna replied. "At seventy degrees, we don't need a coat and can enjoy outdoor activities without having to worry about frostbite."

"Sounds divine." Merry put the phone on speaker and set it on the coffee table.

"It is. But that's not why I called."

"Okay…?"

"I'm still worried about you. I don't want you sitting in that condo by yourself on Christmas and your birthday."

Merry leaned back against the sofa cushions. "And what do you suggest I do instead?"

"Anything. Go to church, visit an outdoor nativity scene, take a drive through that light display at the upscale neighborhood in Melville I told you about, go knock on Paul and Alex's door and ask them to join you for coffee. It doesn't matter what you do—just get out and do something."

Merry leaned back against the sofa cushions and stared at the ceiling. *Do something.* It seemed like excellent advice in theory. Despite Donna's helpful suggestions, she didn't know where to begin. She thought about it so long that Donna "yoohooed" her from the other end of the phone. "Okay, Donna, I promise to do something productive."

"And report back to me when I get home."

"Someone's at the door, Donna. Have a nice Christmas." Merry marveled at how easily little white lies popped out of her mouth these days. She disconnected the phone.

A glance at the clock over the stove explained why her stomach was rumbling. It was almost noon, and she'd never eaten breakfast. She set the tea kettle to boil, then opened the fridge and took out the leftover broccoli soup. It was heating in the microwave when her doorbell actually did ring. Paul, perhaps? Merry couldn't think of anyone else who would stop by on Christmas Eve.

She opened the door, and her jaw dropped when she realized it wasn't her next-door neighbor. There stood Grady, almost completely hidden behind a huge potted poinsettia. Before she could decide what to do— invite him in or make polite excuses to get rid of him— Spookie darted out between her legs.

"No," Merry shouted. "Spookie!"

"I'll get her," Grady said. He set the plant on the small, covered porch and took off after Spookie.

Merry watched, anxiously at first, and then with amusement.

He almost cornered the cat under a bush in front of Merry's front window, and he grabbed at her but missed when she hopped up onto the planter box. They ran a few laps around the mailbox until Spookie settled herself onto Paul's front porch.

The cat probably thought she'd won the game, because by the time he caught up, she was busy grooming herself.

Grady returned the purring cat to Merry.

"Shame on you, Spookie," Merry cooed as she set the cat inside the door. She tried to keep from laughing, but the spectacle of a grown man chasing a playful kitty around a small garden was seared into her brain. She giggled a bit, then burst out laughing.

Pretty soon Grady was chuckling, too, and several minutes passed before they were able to control themselves.

Merry wiped her eyes with the back of her hand. "Sorry about that. She's a handful sometimes." That's when she glanced down at her attire and blushed.

Grady cleared his throat and bent to retrieve the plant. "I brought you a gift. And an invitation."

She admired the beautiful red poinsettia in its decorative green pot, surrounded by professionally arranged moss and a red velvet bow tied around its middle, but she knew she couldn't keep it.

Grady peered into the living room. "Where can I put this?"

"On the porch. Poinsettias are poison for cats.

Dogs, too, for that matter." She opened the door to admit Grady.

He blushed as he set down the plant again before stepping inside. "Sorry, I'm not a pet owner. I just wanted…"

"You didn't know. And it's the thought that counts." Merry smiled. He looked so sheepish over such a small mistake, and her heart almost went out to him. Almost. "What brings you by today? You said something about an invitation?" Was he about to invite her to dinner? On Christmas Eve? Would that be so terrible?

Grady grinned and rocked back on his heels. "Yes. Sorry I didn't call first."

Merry's brow furrowed. "I don't remember giving you my number, and I'm sure I didn't tell you where I live."

"Robin's an easy touch." Grady shrugged as he glanced around her condo. "Nice place, and all decorated, too."

"Thank you." Merry wondered when he'd get to the point. The curiosity was killing her.

He shifted his weight from one foot to the other and poked at an imaginary something on the floor with his toe. "Well, as I'm sure you know, Eli and Robin are off to Hawaii."

"Yes. They stopped by earlier on their way to the airport."

Grady took a deep breath and exhaled slowly. "So…now hear me out…With Eli and Robin gone, I was about to go back to South Bend when I got a call. A holiday invitation for both of us."

Merry's eyes widened. "Us?"

"Since the kids are gone and you don't appear to have plans," Grady said with a subtle head tilt toward her loungewear, "my friends insisted we both come."

"Friends?" She shook her head, thinking she must sound like an idiot to Grady, repeating his words back to him. But this bizarre invitation had come out of nowhere.

"Jane and Arthur Beddington. They just opened a bed and breakfast down in Irvington this fall. Beddington and Breakfast is what they're calling it. Kind of clever, don't you think?"

It was clever actually. Irvington was an old, established neighborhood close to downtown Indianapolis, nearly an hour's drive away. "I haven't bcen down to Irvington in a couple of years, but I love all the antique shops and quaint restaurants."

"Is that a yes?"

"I don't even know what I'm saying yes or no to." The suggestion was outrageous—a holiday with Grady and his friends. Emphasis on *his.*

And yet…What else did she have to do? She promised Donna she wouldn't sit home alone. And what she'd told Eli and Robin about being invited over to Paul and Alex's was just wishful thinking. She shook her head. "I'll have to think about it."

Grady reached for the door. "No time to think. I'll pick you up at four. And pack a bag." He winked and left.

"Grady," she called after him.

With the poinsettia in tow, he waved over his head but didn't look back. He set the plant inside his SUV, started the engine, and drove off.

Merry closed the door and leaned against it,

arguing with herself about the whole idea. Finally, she picked up her phone, determined to text Gradison Williams a firm "no." But she didn't have his number. She'd need to text Robin for it, and Robin was out of reach at the moment. Merry glanced over at Spookie curled up on the sofa. "What just happened?"

Spookie stood, arched her back in a stretch, jumped down, and ran into the bedroom.

Moments later, startled by a loud thud, Merry jumped. What had Spookie gotten into this time? She hurried to the bedroom but stopped at the doorway, gaping in surprise.

Spookie was perched atop her soft-sided overnight bag, which had somehow tumbled to the floor.

Merry ran to the closet and perused the top shelf where she was sure the bag had been securely stored.

The cat couldn't have knocked it down, so Merry was perplexed. Was this a sign she should accept Grady's invitation?

****

Merry shifted the platter of cookies into her left hand and knocked on Paul and Alex's front door. She hadn't called first, so she was relieved when Paul opened the door right away.

"Merry," he said with a smile. "Come in. You're just in time for tea."

She stepped inside, unzipped her down jacket, and took in their lovely condo. Like hers, the front door opened directly into the living space, with the open kitchen to the left and a hallway to the bedroom and bath straight ahead. Unlike hers, though, this condo had a much-larger living room, plus a second bedroom down the hall with its own bath.

Paul and Alex decorated their living room in what designers nowadays called mid-century modern, with bright colors, geometrically-shaped furniture on diminutive walnut legs, and pop art adorning the walls. She smiled at the irony. She had grown up in the nineteen sixties and seventies, when mid-century modern was just, well, modern, and now young people were recreating the style and calling it retro.

Merry marveled at the vintage pink aluminum Christmas tree that stood in the far corner of the living room, festooned with silver ornaments and white lights. Two stockings that looked like someone's grandmother hand-knitted them hung on a faux fireplace mantel next to the tree. One was red and had *Paul* embroidered on the top, and the green one read *Alex.* "I come bearing gifts. Okay, a bribe." Merry handed the plate to Paul as she inhaled the delightful aromas emanating from his kitchen. "Whatever you're baking smells amazing."

"I've got a cake in the oven, a new recipe I might use at work depending on how it turns out." Paul winked, took the platter, and helped himself to a cookie. "Alex and I can't get enough of these." He grinned as he wiped crumbs from his face. "So why do I need to be bribed?"

"I need some advice," Merry said.

Paul set the porcelain platter carefully on the marble kitchen countertop, went to the living room, and plopped himself down on the retro orange sofa. He patted the spot next to him. "How can I help?"

Merry sat where Paul indicated, marveling at how comfortable the sofa was despite being so low to the ground. She fingered the locket Robin gave her and took a couple of deep breaths to calm herself. "I had a visitor a couple of hours ago. My daughter's fiancé's father."

Paul nodded. "So what did Mr…?"

"…Williams. Grady," Merry said.

"So what did Grady want?" Paul gave her an exaggerated wink. "Maybe he heard about your cookies and hoped to get a sample?"

Merry snickered, but before she could answer, Alex burst through the front door with a blast of cold air.

"We have a guest," Paul called out.

"So I see." Alex removed his fur-lined jean jacket and wool scarf and hung them on the metal and wooden coat rack near the door, revealing his blue scrubs and still-attached name tag--Alex Gordon, R.N. "Merry Christmas, Merry." He laughed at his own joke. "Sorry."

Merry laughed. "Not the first time I've heard that. Slow in the ER I hope?"

"Blessedly slow. Just a kid with a sugar-overdose bellyache and a mom going into labor. Somehow that seemed fitting on Christmas Eve." He grinned. "Can I offer you anything? Tea?" Alex cast a glance at Paul. "My husband seems to have forgotten his manners."

"I offered," Paul said with a sniff. "Sort of."

Merry shifted around so she could see Alex. "I just popped over with more of my Christmas sugar cookies, hoping to pick your brains for advice."

Alex went to the kitchen and set the tea kettle on the stove. "I'm listening," he called. He spied the plate of cookies and began to nibble on one. "Mmmm."

"I just love to advise the lovelorn." Paul tilted his head at Merry's attire. "And we didn't do all that shopping to impress Spookie."

She narrowed her eyes. "I'm not lovelorn." But she self-consciously smoothed out an imaginary wrinkle in her new skinny jeans, tugged at the sleeves of her burgundy cardigan sweater, and toyed with the locket. "Grady asked me to join him and some of his friends in Irvington for the holidays."

The tea kettle whistled. Alex reappeared in the living room, balancing a lime green tea pot on a tray with three porcelain Christmas mugs. "Sugar?" He poured tea into all three.

Merry took a sip and waved away the sugar bowl. "Doesn't need sugar. Must be one of those special Christmas blends. I taste cinnamon, nutmeg, and a hint of cloves." She took another sip and savored the delicious spices mingled together in her mug.

"So this Grady guy?" Paul took a sip of his own tea. "I know your children are engaged, but just how close are the two of you?"

Merry swallowed her tea and shook her head. "I only met him for the first time a few days ago. He flirted with me at a bar, if you can imagine. And then the next day at school, he turned up to give a presentation about the so-called improvements his charter school will make when they take over our school next month." She rolled her eyes. "Let's say we didn't exactly hit it off."

"Awkward," Paul muttered. "So what changed?"

Merry gave that some thought as she took another sip of tea. "He helped out with the school's Good Samaritan drive last weekend. And then he cooked a family dinner at my daughter's house. His lasagna was amazing."

"So he's a helpful guy with a flair for Italian cuisine," Alex said, "but a corporate shark bent on school destruction. Quite the resume." He settled into one of the adjacent gray armchairs, blew on his tea, and took a tentative sip. "Do you already have holiday plans? You could always decline his last-minute invitation."

"That's just it," Merry said. "I don't. Robin and Eli are probably in Hawaii by now, and my best friend Donna is with her family in Texas. I'm at loose ends."

Paul had a mischievous twinkle in his eye. "So what did he suggest, and is he cute enough to accept?"

Merry blushed. "He said his friends have a new B and B in Irvington, Beddington and Breakfast, and that I was invited. Why? I don't know." She took another sip of the delicious tea.

Paul retrieved his phone from the coffee table and punched at it. "It's a real place." He showed the phone to Merry. "Owned by Jane and Arthur Beddington, and it just opened a couple of months ago." He pointed to the online posting. "Says it's a renovated, nineteenth-century farmhouse, situated in the heart of Irvington."

Paul nodded as he handed over his phone. "Cute place."

Merry studied the photo on Paul's phone. "It *is* attractive."

"Good reviews from the few guests they've had." Paul set down the phone. "So what's the problem?"

"The problem is, I barely know Grady, and I don't know his friends at all. But if I stay here, Christmas is looking like microwave leftovers and Hallmark movies snuggled up with a cat."

Alex and Paul exchanged glances. "Go," Alex said.

Merry sat with that for a moment. "And speaking of Spookie…"

Paul waved that away. "Don't give her a second thought. I'll take good care of that adorable kitty."

Merry glanced at the nineteen-sixties-era wall clock that looked just like one her parents had when she was a child, with its metal spokes and wooden balls on the tips. Three p.m. If she was going to Irvington with Grady in an hour, she needed to get home and pack.

"Merry," Paul said, reaching for her hand. "All kidding aside, he's offering a pleasant couple of days and a chance to meet new people in a safe environment. Where's the harm?"

"When you put it like that…" She hesitated. "But you probably have your own holiday plans. Are you sure looking after Spookie isn't an imposition?"

"No imposition," Paul assured her. "We're having some friends over for Christmas brunch, but we can easily pop over and take care of the kitty. Or maybe I'll bring her over here."

"Thank you so much." Merry stood, pulled a key out of her pocket, and handed it to Paul. "The cat food is in the pantry, and treats are in the drawer next to the stove."

"Spookie will be spoiled rotten." Paul opened the door for Merry and gave her a hug, a twinkle in his eye. "Have a wonderful holiday. And I want details when you get back."

As Merry left their condo, she wondered what those details might include.

Chapter Eight
Monday, December 24

Butterflies danced in Merry's stomach as she answered her doorbell at four p.m.

"You ready?" Grady smiled and blew on his hands as he stepped inside.

She slipped into her coat and reached for her overnight bag and purse. Qualms about this whole crazy scheme kept tumbling through her head, but she reminded herself that she had nothing better to do over Christmas, and Spookie would be well cared for. In fact, Paul had just come over and snatched the kitty, who purred all the way out the door.

She pulled her phone out of her pocket and perused it quickly for any new texts. Nothing. "Yes, I think so."

"Expecting a call?" Grady asked.

Merry put away her phone. "I keep hoping to hear from Robin, telling me she and Eli are on the beach in Honolulu right now."

"Lucky them." He shrugged. "I'm sure they'll send a text, probably while we're driving down to Irvington."

Merry snapped her fingers. "That reminds me." She hurried into the kitchen, opened the pantry, and pulled out a plastic container of her Christmas sugar cookies. "I want to take some of my world-famous…okay, family favorite…sugar cookies. I didn't have time to buy a hostess gift, so these will have to do."

Grady wiggled an eyebrow. "If you ask me, they'll do nicely."

Merry felt a tingle down her spine when Grady handed her into the passenger side of his SUV, that same tingle she'd felt when their hands touched at Robin's, and then again at the coffee shop. She shook her head. *Your fingers must be numb from the cold.*

While fastening her seatbelt, she wracked her brain for polite, generic conversation. Something that didn't involve the unpleasant changes about to take place at Thomas Belford Prep, or the sad fact that she'd never spent a Christmas away from Robin. "It's very cold today." *Weather? It's December in Indiana. Is that the best you can do?*

"Dashboard says it's fifteen degrees," Grady said as he drove out of her neighborhood and onto the main road.

"Do you like...?" Grady asked as Merry asked, "What sort of...?"

They laughed, then Grady said, "You first."

"I was going to ask what sort of music you listen to in the car. I know it's quite the drive from South Bend to, um..." She let *Belford* drift away.

"Yes." Grady blushed. "Sometimes traffic is awful, so I find a little Mozart soothes the savage beast."

Merry cringed at Grady's mangling of the famous quote.

"But since it's Christmas Eve, I'm sure we can find some holiday tunes." He fumbled with the car's radio until he landed on a local station playing Christmas music. Grady glanced over. "Now that it's out there, shall we discuss the elephant in the room? Or rather, the car?"

"Elephant?" Merry wasn't as perplexed as she hoped she sounded, but Grady was right. It was just hanging there.

"I know you think my company goes marauding all over the country, on missions to search and destroy public schools. But that's not the case. We only go by invitation, and your principal invited us."

Merry's jaw dropped. "She did?"

"She did."

"But when your company goes into a school, you already have a plan to, uh…"

"…to help the school get back on its feet," Grady finished. "Financially, and academically, too, if that's part of the problem." He furrowed his brow. "Didn't Dr. Alexander explain our mission?"

"No, she kept it hush-hush all week and then just sprang it on the faculty in that meeting." Merry shook her head, amazed at her own naiveté. All this time she'd been blaming Grady and his company for taking advantage of Belford Prep's vulnerability, when in fact the principal, with the blessing of the school board of course, had reached out.

The problem couldn't be solved now, and anyway, Merry needed to sit with her principal's subterfuge for a bit. She stared out the window as they drove down Interstate 69, until it transitioned into Interstate 465 Southbound, and enjoyed the popular Christmas songs playing on the radio. "My neighbor Googled this bed and breakfast we're going to," Merry said, breaking the silence, "but since you know the owners, maybe you can tell me more about them."

"Jane and Arthur Beddington. It was always their dream to open a bed and breakfast. They retired from their careers in South Bend last spring, bought a Victorian farmhouse that could only be called a fixer, and had it restored."

"So you know this couple well?"

Grady kept his focus on the road, not making eye contact with Merry. "Jane and I met in college. I've known Arthur a shorter time, but he's a great guy."

"But why Indianapolis? Why not South Bend? Or Chicago?"

"To be closer to…" Grady's voice trailed off as he signaled a lane change and headed for the Washington Street exit. He flipped on his headlights, because it was already getting dark, typical for a late December afternoon.

Merry marveled at the variety of older homes dotting the roads—everything from late nineteenth century to post-World War II. Some had no exterior lighting, some had beautiful and festive twinkling Christmas lights, and many boasted lighted Christmas trees prominently displayed in a front window. For whatever reason, the Beddingtons had chosen Indianapolis to open their bed and breakfast, and Merry had to admit historic Irvington was the perfect location.

"'Silver bells…'" sang a crooner on the radio.

"…'Silver bells," Grady chimed in with a surprisingly clear baritone. He glanced over at the passenger seat and gave Merry a playful elbow nudge.

She smiled and joined in, a bit off-key, and together, they finished the song. Since it was Christmas Eve, traffic on the freeway and the side streets was light, so the drive from Belford had taken them less than the anticipated hour.

Grady turned onto a residential street that would have been completely dark but for the brightly lit Christmas decorations on some of the houses. He drove slowly to the end of the street to a large, double-wide lot, and pulled into a marked parking space in the oversized driveway. "This is it." Grady cut the engine.

Merry peered out the window. The old house was charming. It was a two-story, frame farmhouse with a wraparound front porch sporting a white porch swing, and the wooden siding had been painted yellow with white accents on the gingerbread latticework. A Christmas wreath adorned the front door, and faux candles burned brightly in all five windows facing the street. Well-trimmed but snow-covered bushes graced either side of the main entrance, and a sign in the yard painted with a Victorian flair read Beddington and Breakfast.

"Has this always been a B and B?"

Grady shook his head as he got out of the car. "It was a farmhouse back when this area was rural, then a private residence, then abandoned for years until Jane and Arthur bought it from the city." He retrieved Merry's overnight bag from the trunk, along with his own backpack, and opened her car door. "You ready?"

She could hear raucous piano music emanating from inside the house, causing her stomach butterflies to return. She hesitated. "They're obviously having a party. I don't want to intrude."

Grady smiled as he took Merry's hand and helped her out of the SUV. "You're not intruding. You were invited. Come on." He led her up the two wooden front steps, opened the unlocked door, and stuck in his head.

"Hello?"

The piano music continued unabated, someone pounding out a rendition of "Deck the Halls."

Closing the door behind them, Merry followed Grady into the tiny, makeshift guest check-in area, with an old-fashioned lectern and handwritten ledger book, festooned for the holidays with evergreen garlands. Off to her right, she saw a large, open living room with a blazing fire in the hearth. She felt a sense of warmth permeating the house, both literally and figuratively, and decided she liked it here, even if she didn't know Grady's friends.

He set her overnight bag and his own bulging backpack on the floor near the lectern. "Helloo!"

The music stopped, and an attractive woman who appeared to be about Merry's age swept in from the living room. She was medium height with shoulder-length dark hair, dressed in jeans and a Christmas sweatshirt. The reindeer's nose on her shirt blinked a bright red.

Merry smiled at the thought of her own tacky Christmas sweatshirt, the one she'd worn when she first met Grady.

"Keith." The woman gave him a quick hug.

"Keith?" Merry glanced at Grady.

Grady winked at Merry. "Merry, this is Jane Beddington, proprietor of this quaint establishment. I told you she and I go way back."

Jane smiled and extended her hand. "You must be Merry Halliday. It's a pleasure to finally meet you."

Finally? Merry wondered what Grady had been telling Jane about her. She shook Jane's extended hand. "Thanks for having me last minute."

Jane somehow looked familiar. Something about her eyes, framed in thick dark lashes, reminded her of someone, but she couldn't quite put her finger on it.

"Arthur?" Jane called out to her husband.

A silver-haired gentleman, who appeared to be a few years older than Jane, joined them. "Well, look who's here." Arthur shook hands with Grady. "And Merry? We've been looking forward to meeting you."

A little curly-haired boy about five or six years old dashed into the entryway, put his hands on his hips, and stomped his feet. "Gramma Janie, Daddy just threw another log on the fire."

Jane got down to the child's eye level. "What's wrong with that, Trey? It's cold outside."

"How's Santa gonna get down the chimney if it's on fire?"

Jane smiled and patted his head. "Don't worry, hon. Santa has his ways." She turned the little boy around to face Merry. "Trey, we have a guest. This is Mrs. Halliday. And, Merry, Trey Beddington is our grandson."

"Nice to meet you, Trey." Merry offered her hand to shake.

"Hi." The little boy gave her a quick, limp shake before darting off.

Merry suddenly felt very self-conscious. These lovely people were enjoying their holiday with family, and she was nothing but a hotel guest. A guest of a guest, actually. "Please don't let me interrupt your family celebration. Just point me to my room."

"You're family, too," Jane said.

Merry blinked. "Well, that's certainly kind of you to say, but…"

Grady held up a hand to stop her. "Merry," he said with a twinkle in his eye, "she's right. You *are* family. Jane is Eli's mother."

Merry turned to Grady, eyes wide. "Why on earth didn't you mention this before?"

Grady rocked back on his heels and grinned a wicked smile. "I wanted to surprise you?"

"Mission accomplished." *More like blind-sided.*

Naturally, Merry had wanted to meet Robin's future mother-in-law, and she knew Eli's mother and stepfather lived somewhere in Indianapolis, but now it all made sense—why the Beddingtons had chosen to move from South Bend to Indianapolis, and why Jane reminded her of someone. Eli, of course.

Merry relaxed, knowing she really did have a connection to this family. "It's wonderful to finally meet you. I think the world of your son."

Jane wrapped her in a warm bear hug. "Sorry for the subterfuge, but Keith—Grady—swore me to secrecy. Let me show you to your room. You can freshen up and then join our unruly Christmas Eve." Jane winked at Grady. "And you don't want to miss Keith's rendition of *Silent Night.*"

Merry retrieved her overnight bag from the floor where Grady dropped it and reached inside it. "I know it's not a traditional hostess gift, but I'm pretty renowned for my Christmas cookies."

Jane popped the plastic lid and took a whiff. "They smell delicious. Real vanilla?"

Merry nodded.

"Yum. Arthur, can you take these to the kitchen for me?" She handed the cookies to her husband, who popped one in his mouth.

Merry followed Jane up a staircase that, judging by how narrow it was, must have been original to the house. They passed several closed doors, all with the historic Greek revival scrolls intact, and walked to the end of the brightly lit hallway.

Jane opened the door with a key hanging on a lanyard around her neck and flipped on the lights.

Merry was delighted. "This looks like the cover of a magazine." The decorations were modern but with a hint of vintage charm. A queen-sized bed piled high with pastel-colored throw pillows and a coordinating green nightstand with a faux Tiffany lamp were the centerpieces of the room. In lieu of a built-in closet, an antique cherrywood armoire with full-length mirror stood in a corner. White peonies formed patterns in the green wallpaper which matched the bed's coverlet, and white lace curtains hung gracefully at the window which overlooked the front of the house.

Jane parted the curtains for a peek. The corner street lamp and the neighbors' twinkling outdoor holiday lights illuminated the front lawn. "I'm hoping we have a white Christmas."

Merry peered out. "I haven't listened to a weather report since school let out for the holidays, but that would be nice."

"A bit of snow on Christmas is always welcome." Jane indicated a door just to the left of the window. "Your private bath. Towels, bathrobe, scented soaps, shampoo. If you need anything, just dial zero on the house phone, or better yet, feel free to come downstairs and help yourself." She withdrew the lanyard and room key from around her neck and handed it to Merry. "I'll let you get settled in."

"Jane? I want to thank you again for having me. I really was at loose ends this holiday."

Jane smiled. "I haven't gotten to know Robin as well as I'd like, but she's a lovely young woman, and she makes my son very happy. I'm thrilled to finally meet her mother." She opened the door and let herself out.

Merry took her toiletries from her overnight bag and placed them on the bathroom counter, and then hung up trousers and a crepe blouse. Sweaters wouldn't need to be unpacked for the duration of her short stay, so she placed the half-filled bag on the bottom shelf of the armoire. She started to toss her handbag in after it but realized she forgot to check her phone on the way down from Belford. Merry sighed as she perused her texts. Still no word from Robin.

They're probably taking a romantic walk on the beach. The idea made her smile.

She swiped at her hair with a comb, freshened her lipstick, and considered the burgundy cardigan sweater she'd been wearing most of the day. Should she change? She glanced at her reflection in the mirror and decided it looked fine. Merry closed and locked the door to her room and retraced her steps, following the sound of laughter and a loud piano rendition of "Jingle Bells."

"Ah, there you are." Grady waved her into the room.

Merry scouted out the large living space. Nineteenth-century farmhouses traditionally had smaller rooms that could be heated by a wood stove or fireplace, so Jane and Arthur must have added on to the original structure.

The Christmas tree was massive, taking up an entire corner of the room and reaching all the way to the ceiling, heavily adorned with festive twinkling lights and an eclectic assortment of ornaments. A large angel sat atop, smiling down from her ten-foot perch. The focal point of the room was the red brick fireplace, with a large wooden mantel currently home to four mismatched Christmas stockings. The firewood in the hearth was ablaze with heat and crackling pine cones, causing Merry to smile at little Trey's concern for Santa's safety. She waved at Jane across the room.

Jane stood, hands on hips, surveying the large, fir Christmas tree. She waved back at Merry. "Help yourself to refreshments," she called out. "We have hot chocolate or coffee in the kitchen." She stood on tiptoe to reach an unlit bulb on the tree, gave it a twist, and nodded as it flickered on.

Merry followed the tilt of Jane's head to the antique dining table, all but groaning under the weight of so many treats. She selected cheese and crackers, a helping from the vegetable tray, and a variety of Christmas cookies. She beamed with pleasure at the sight of her own cookies, which were prominently displayed front and center on a holiday plate. Next to it sat a tea service on a silver tray, surrounded by china cups and saucers.

Merry's stomach rumbled, reminding her she hadn't eaten since she heated that soup before going to Paul and Alex's. She poured herself a cup of orange pekoe tea and gingerly sipped the hot beverage, the citrus-y scent wafting up her nose. She was so hungry she ate standing up.

"Aren't you glad I talked you into coming?"

Merry nodded at Grady as she swallowed the last bite of her cookie. She glanced around for a place to set down her now-empty dishes.

"Here, allow me."

It was like Grady could read her mind. He snatched one of her cookies off the table and moaned with pleasure, munching away as he whisked her dishes into the kitchen.

Merry wandered over to the tree. She gently fingered several of the ornaments, each from a different year, and each featuring a specific theme—first day of school, a soccer win, Eli's high school graduation, even a scroll commemorating his law degree. Colored glass ornaments that could be bought at any discount store were woven in among the memory-filled family ornaments. But a tiny, faded homemade book hanging from a ribbon caught Merry's attention. The outside featured a hand-drawn decorated tree, and inside, written in a child's hand, read *Merry Christmas to Mom*. Her heart melted.

"He made that for Jane in first grade," Grady said as he returned to her side.

"It's very sweet. It reminds me of an ornament Robin made me when she was in elementary school. A red musical cleft, because she was in the children's choir, and in green letters she wrote," Merry raised her fingers in air quotes, "*Merry* Christmas. Sort of a play on words." Her eyes misted over.

"You okay?" Grady asked.

Merry nodded. "Just thinking I'd like to wish Robin a Merry Christmas."

Grady was silent a moment as he turned his attention back to the tree. "I understand. I miss Eli, too."

Merry felt a pang of empathy for Grady. "Do you have any other family? Besides Eli?" She knew Grady and Jane had amicably divorced when Eli was in elementary school, but after that, the story was a blank.

Grady shook his head. "My parents, Eli's grandparents, died a few years ago. And I was always so busy…" He sighed. "Make that too busy for relationships that didn't involve a corporate merger."

Merry nodded, because if she was being honest, her current life revolved around her teaching career and a black rescue cat named Spookie. "I'm glad you insisted I come." She waved her hand around the room. "Jane and Arthur have done a marvelous job of making this place homey and festive."

"Okay, everyone!" Jane clapped her hands for attention and motioned everyone to the piano. "It's time to sing Trey off to bed." She leaned down to the yawning child and gave him an exaggerated wink. "Santa won't visit until you're asleep."

Grady and Merry made their way across the room to join Trey and another young man as they gathered around the piano. "Merry," Grady said, indicating the handsome young man in jeans, t-shirt, and a gaudy Christmas tie, "this is Arthur's son, Artie."

Merry smiled as she made the connection. Arthur, Artie, and, of course, Arthur the third. Trey. She offered her hand to shake. "Nice to meet you. I'm Robin Halliday's mother."

Artie shook her hand. "A pleasure."

Arthur sat at the piano, ran his fingers across the keyboard, and played a few bars of "We Wish You a Merry Christmas." He sang the first line, and everyone else joined in the chorus, while Grady chimed in with a pleasant harmony.

Merry was impressed yet again with his beautiful voice.

As the group finished the last stanza, Artie took a yawning Trey by the hand and led him up the stairs.

In the meantime, Arthur played a few introductory bars of the classic Christmas carol, "Silent Night."

Merry was spellbound as Grady sang all the verses by heart.

Jane crisscrossed the room, collecting an empty cup here, a used plate there, stacking them one on top of the other.

Merry gathered some empty mugs of hot chocolate and followed Jane into the kitchen. "Where shall I put these?"

Jane gently set down her armload of dishes on the granite countertop and tilted her head to the island. "There is fine. But you're our guest, so I don't want you working."

"Nonsense. 'Many hands make light work' as they say."

"No, I insist," Jane said. "Please, go enjoy the rest of the evening."

Merry placed her hands on her hips. "I'll go, but I reserve the right to help with Christmas dinner tomorrow."

Jane opened the dishwasher and began loading plates. "We'll see."

Merry reluctantly returned to the family room.

Arthur closed the piano lid, switched off the overhead chandelier, and dimmed the table lamp. "Think I'll leave on the tree," he said, perhaps to her, perhaps to himself. He nodded as he headed down the hall.

Merry assumed he headed to the owners' suite. "Goodnight," she called after him.

"Walk you home?" Grady asked, coming up behind her.

"What?"

He winked. "My room's just up the hallway from yours." He offered his arm.

Merry only hesitated a second before linking her arm through his. "Lead the way." Up the narrow stairs they went, Merry acutely aware of their close proximity. When they arrived at her door at the end of the hallway, she unlocked it before turning to say goodnight.

Grady opened his mouth to speak, and then closed it again.

"Well, goodnight," she said.

Grady leaned in. "Thanks again for accepting my last-minute invitation. See you in the morning," he whispered.

For a brief moment, Merry thought he was going to kiss her, but instead, he squeezed her hand and walked away. She went into her room and closed the door, her heart pounding.

Chapter Nine
Tuesday, December 25

Merry popped open her eyes, a dream lingering in her mind. Something about Bert on a sidewalk just out of reach, Robin too far away to hear her, and then suddenly, Grady appeared by her side.

Too many sweets and all that tea before bedtime. After all, it was Christmas morning, and a dream about her late husband and her daughter made sense. But the part about Grady? Although he'd been kind to her the last few days—perhaps kinder than she'd been to him if she was being honest—he had no reason to stand by her side. Merry wondered if Grady had sneaked into her dreams because he "rescued" her from a lonely holiday.

And the part about Robin being out of reach?

Even before Bert's death, Robin had established her own holiday rituals. She would come over for brunch, exchange gifts, and they'd watch a holiday film on TV. Robin would promise to see Merry on her birthday and then hurry off to meet friends. Robin's routine didn't change after her dad died, but last year instead of friends, she hurried off to meet Eli.

Merry glanced at the bedside clock. It was after nine o'clock. Sun streamed through the bedroom window, and the smell of sausage and pastries coming from the kitchen reminded her she was hungry. She yawned, stretched, and sat up in bed. A quick glance at the frost on the window told her the snow Jane predicted had arrived. The wind was still blowing and rustling trees, and the hardwood floor felt cold to her bare feet. Hurrying into the bathroom, she lingered a bit too long under the warm shower before wrapping herself in the plush pink towel provided for her use. Merry applied her makeup with great care. *Who am I trying to impress?* Her new friends Jane and Arthur, she told herself. Of course.

She opened the bedroom armoire and rummaged through her overnight bag, considering which outfit best set off her newly-styled auburn hair. She settled on the dark green, scoop-neck cable-knit sweater Paul had picked, paired it with thick black leggings, and stepped into her tan, knee-high leather boots. After adding the locket and earrings Robin gave her, she surveyed her look in the armoire's mirror and hoped she was prepared for whatever this day might bring.

Merry planned to go outside for a walk to give Jane and Arthur's family time to finish opening gifts, but a rumble in her belly told her she had to eat something first. She cringed at the creaky stairs, hoping she wasn't disturbing the family. She stopped on the last step and craned her neck around the corner, peering into the large living room.

The scene reminded her of Robin's childhood—toys scattered everywhere, torn wrapping paper and ribbons tossed on the floor. Laughter filled the room as Arthur and Artie, both sprawled on the floor, played a board game with Trey.

In the kitchen, Merry found Jane up to her elbows in dirty dishes and pots and pans. A quick glance around told her Jane was both cleaning up from breakfast and in the early stages of preparing Christmas dinner. "Merry Christmas. Do you need any help?"

Jane glanced over her shoulder and smiled. "Merry Christmas to you! I'm glad you were able to sleep in. Trey was so excited this morning that he woke up Artie before six. Things got pretty loud."

Merry smiled, remembering when Robin was that excited to see what Santa had brought.

"I saved you some breakfast in the fridge. Just nuke it up." Jane pointed to the microwave over the stove.

Merry opened the refrigerator to find an egg and sausage casserole, a recipe she knew required a lot of preparation. "When did you have time to do all this?"

Jane returned to the dirty pots and pans in her sink, squirting more dishwashing liquid into the steaming water. "A couple of days ago. That particular recipe freezes well."

Merry scooped a generous portion of the casserole onto a porcelain plate and set it in the microwave. She scouted around the kitchen for toast or…

"Fresh sliced fruit in the fridge, and sweet rolls on that platter under the Christmas napkin."

Merry laughed. "It's like you could read my mind." The microwave dinged; she extracted the plate and helped herself to a cinnamon roll and a generous serving of fruit.

"Coffee?" Jane pushed a Christmas mug with an embossed green tree toward her.

"Yes, thank you."

Jane poured her a cup. "Milk or sugar?"

Merry shook her head and took a sip of the hazelnut-flavored coffee. "Doesn't need a thing." She glanced around the cluttered kitchen. "Where should I…?"

"Oh, sorry about the mess. You can sit in the dining room."

Merry gathered her plate, coffee, and a rolled napkin with silverware from a basket on the kitchen island. "Don't forget I offered to help with Christmas dinner," she called from the dining room. She sat and tucked into the savory casserole.

"I said, 'we'll see,'" Jane called back.

****

Coat on, stocking cap pulled tightly over her ears, and scarf tied snuggly about her neck, Merry ventured out. Yes, it was cold, but the sunshine and cloudless sky created a beautiful clear morning. The frozen icicles, dangling from tree limbs, sparkled and danced in the sunlight. The wind had died down, and if she kept moving, she didn't notice the cold.

The snowfall had been light enough that it didn't completely cover the sidewalks or impede her journey. She reveled in the quiet solitude, the only sound the occasional thud of snow falling off a tree or roof. Unfamiliar with the neighborhood, she strolled aimlessly along, admiring the beautifully maintained, early-twentieth-century homes.

A woman walking a dog passed her on the sidewalk. "Merry Christmas," the woman said with a wave.

Just then an adventuresome squirrel, its mouth full of fallen acorns, darted in front of the dog's path. The woman reined in the leash to keep the pooch from giving chase.

Merry smiled and walked on.

"You must be cold."

She turned. "Grady!"

He hurried to catch up. "I slept in, so I missed you at breakfast. Jane said she thought you'd gone for a walk."

Even with gloves on, her hands were getting cold, so she shoved them into her coat pockets for warmth. "I offered to help start dinner, but Jane shooed me out of the kitchen."

"Mind if I join you?"

The two of them walked along in companionable silence until they reached a crossroads in the sidewalk. To the right was a business district with a coffee shop and stores, all closed for the holiday, and to the left were more historic homes.

"Which way?" Merry shivered. "Or should we just go back?"

"Want to see something?" Grady pointed to the path that veered off to the left.

Merry shaded her eyes and followed his gaze. "Something…what? Grady, I've been out here a while, and my toes are getting numb."

"I'm betting you'll think it's worth it." He ducked his head and took off in the direction of…whatever.

Merry glanced back towards the warmth of the bed and breakfast, sighed, and followed along.

Grady seemed to know of a path, mostly hidden under the snow, and he strolled confidently toward his destination. It didn't take them long. "This is it," he said with an arm flourish.

Merry studied the structure before them, which was partially hidden among the trees. It appeared to be an old church, an A-frame white clapboard. The structure boasted a large, black, double-wide door, stained glass windows on each side of the door, a bell tower on top, a large well-kept yard in front, and a modern parking lot off to the side.

"I found it last fall when I visited Jane and Arthur after they settled in here. This was an old Methodist church back when Indianapolis was a new town—early eighteen twenties or so—but it was long abandoned and falling down."

"It's beautiful," Merry whispered.

"A few years ago, an investor bought it, restored it, and turned it into a wedding chapel. Outside it's still quaint, but inside it has all the modern conveniences, and there's a waiting list for young couples wanting to get married here." Grady grinned. "I looked online."

Merry walked up the three wooden steps and peered into one of the stained-glass windows, unable to see much through the distorted colors. The thought crossed her mind how beautiful Robin would look walking down the aisle in a vintage chapel like this one, but she shook it off. Robin and Eli had already booked a large venue for their hundred or more guests. Merry knew Robin would never agree to a place this small.

Grady reached around her to try the door handle. "Would you look at that?" He opened the door a crack and peeked in.

Merry hesitated. "Are we trespassing?"

Grady shrugged. "Maybe they left it open for passersby to drop in on Christmas Day. Anyway, it's cold out here, and there's no one around, so…" He held the door wide to let her pass in front of him.

Merry blew on her cold hands and stomped her feet as she stepped inside the warm building, glancing up to see modern air ducts conducting the heat. It looked like the set of a "Little House on the Prairie" film, with wooden pews on either side of the aisle. An old-fashioned podium on a raised dais stood in the center—equipped with a sound system for the twenty-first century—and a large cross hung on the wall behind it. Bright sunlight streamed through the floor-to-ceiling, stained-glass windows on either side of the chapel, giving Merry a sense of awe and peace.

Grady took a seat in a pew and patted the spot next to him. "I've visited Jane and Arthur's B and B a few times and always admired this chapel, but I've never been in it." He glanced around. "It's very, um…"

"Quaint?" Merry offered.

Grady nodded.

"I was wondering." Merry sat where Grady indicated. "Since you've obviously spent time at Jane and Arthur's, why did you get a downtown hotel room?"

Grady laughed. "My ex-wife and I are friendly, and Arthur's a great guy, but it's Christmas, and they have their own family. The hotel suited my needs."

"But you stayed last night at Beddington and Breakfast."

"Jane insisted, because after Eli and Robin left, I was planning to go back to South Bend for Christmas. I've still got the hotel room, though, and I'll stay there tonight."

Merry had no idea what it was like to be divorced, but she knew all too well about being single and lacking family. She was an only child, and her parents both passed away years ago. That left Bert and Robin, and now just Robin. She took in her surroundings, really looking around—first the altar, then the vaulted roof, and finally the hymnals tucked into shelves under the pew in front of her. She pulled out a copy and thumbed through it, randomly landing on a hymn. "This is a Day of New Beginnings." She'd never heard that one, but the lyrics seemed to be speaking to her. Without her glasses, she had to squint as she read aloud, "Step from the past……"

Grady peered over her shoulder. "Oh, I love that hymn." He sang a few bars.

A chill went down Merry's spine. Was it Grady's singing? Or was it something awakening inside her like the hymn suggested? Her early morning dream of Grady being by her side flooded back. She closed the book and returned it to its shelf. "You have a beautiful voice."

"Thanks. I used to sing in the church choir when Eli was growing up."

His mention of Eli reminded her she still hadn't heard from Robin. She pulled her phone from her coat pocket and scrolled through her messages. "Have you gotten any texts from the kids?"

Grady furrowed his brow. "Come to think of it, no."

"I've sent Robin several texts," Merry said, "but no response. It's been over twenty-four hours, and by now, I thought she would have sent some beach photos or something."

Grady pulled out his phone and checked for messages. "Nothing from Eli either." He shook his head and returned the phone to the clip on his belt. "What time is it in Hawaii anyway?"

"It's five hours earlier. They're probably just

waking up." Merry couldn't put her finger on it, but she felt uneasy about Robin's radio silence. It wasn't like her. "Surely, we'll hear from them later today. Right?"

He patted her hand. "Definitely. Eli always replies to my texts."

Merry's hand tingled at his innocent pat, but then her mind wandered—to Grady and Eli's close relationship, then to what might be keeping her daughter from replying to texts, and finally, to next week. Rather than make eye contact, she glanced up at the wooden ceiling rafters. "I've had time to think about what you told me, about our principal contacting your charter school."

Grady turned sideways in the pew and leaned his right elbow on the wooden back. "And…?"

Merry swallowed hard. "I hate that she didn't give the faculty a heads-up, but we're adults. I'm mostly worried about the students."

Grady furrowed his brow. "Why would you be worried?"

Merry turned sideways in the seat to face him. "I've read about charter schools and talked to colleagues whose schools were taken over by them. The kids all dress alike, can't speak out of turn, and march up and down the hallways like little robots. The joy is sucked out of the school day, not to mention the kids' lives. Their extra-curriculars get cancelled in favor of tutoring so they'll pass their standardized tests."

"Kind of an exaggeration, don't you think?" Grady took her hand. "Merry."

She tried to pull away.

But he held on tight. "Merry. You're wrong. Yes, Lake City Prep focuses on academics, but it's not a military academy."

She sighed. "Maybe not, but since this whole plan was dumped on us last minute, none of us knows what to expect. Donna read your business card and said she was definitely seeing"—Merry put up air quotes—"'RED.'"

"Really?" Grady scrunched his brow, but then his face lit up with a grin. He chuckled. Then he laughed. And finally he guffawed.

Merry lifted an eyebrow. "That seems funny to you?"

Grady cleared his throat, took a deep breath, and wiped away an errant tear as he finally stopped laughing. "Responsible Educational Directives. I can't believe I never noticed the acronym before." He let one last chuckle escape.

Merry smiled in spite of herself. "Either by design or inadvertent, there it is."

Grady gave her hand a squeeze before releasing it and walked to the window, which was awash in sunlight. "When Dr. Alexander contacted us, she said the school was mere months away from shutting down due to a lack of funding."

"What?" Merry shook her head as she joined him by the window. "The building's old and in need of repairs, and we've lost students to the new high school across town. But I can't believe they'd just close it."

Grady shrugged. "I guess they would if it's cheaper than doing a costly renovation."

She winced. "It's the neighborhood school, steeped in tradition. The huge auditorium, the historic gymnasium…"

He turned to face her. "And it has an offer from a

113

condo developer once it's vacated."

Merry gasped. This was too much to absorb, and she didn't want to break down and cry in front of Grady. "I have to go." She buttoned her coat, wrapped her scarf around her neck, pulled on her gloves, and hurried to the exit.

"Merry, wait!"

She kept walking. She needed distance from Grady and all the emotions he stirred inside her.

****

Merry sailed back into the B and B. Her anger— not at Grady, but at Dr. Alexander's subterfuge—plus her brisk walk back, kept her from feeling the chill. She unfurled her knitted scarf, stuffed her gloves in her coat pocket, hung it on the coat rack in the entryway, and headed into the family room. She warmed her hands in front of the roaring fire, and after a few calming breaths, she felt her anger subside.

"Merry Christmas!" Trey giggled as he ran across the family room and tugged on her wrist.

She leaned down. "Merry Christmas to you, too, Trey. Was Santa good to you?"

"Oh, yeah! He brought me a land rover, a new board game, a nerf football, and..." The little boy grinned. "Hey, ya got any more of those cookies?"

Merry sat on the sofa, leaned her elbows on her knees, and spoke directly to him. "I'm a guest here, but I could ask your grandmother if she'd let me bake some more."

"Yay! Hi, Mr. Williams!" Trey ran back to the tree and dove into his pile of toys.

Merry glanced up and realized Grady was standing behind her, his laptop tucked under his arm. She blushed. "Sorry I stormed out of the chapel like that."

"I want to show you something." Grady dragged over an ottoman and set the laptop on it, sat on the sofa next to Merry, and scrolled around on the screen. "Here's the email Dr. Alexander sent me back in October."

Merry fished out her glasses and read it through.

Dear Mr. Williams:

Our small town high school is in desperate financial straits. Over the last few years, several large businesses closed, and families have moved away. We currently only have about four hundred students left. The building itself is in need of major repairs. Absent any other financial solution, the School Board will be forced to close the building at the end of this school year, move some of the remaining students into the nearby middle school for half days, and the rest to the over-crowded, newer high school across town.

In order to preserve our historic building, I propose we partner with Lake City Prep and convert Thomas Belford Preparatory High School into a charter school. Please review the attached spreadsheet. Time is of the essence, as these difficult decisions must be made before the start of second semester.

Sincerely,

Dr. Shirley Alexander, Principal

Cc: Dr. Albert Casey, School Board President

Merry read and reread the principal's email. She slumped back into the sofa cushions, feeling queasy. "Bah Humbug from the School Board. A bunch of Scrooges if you ask me."

Grady scrolled around on the laptop and opened a spreadsheet, turning it for her to see. "This is the biggest concern," he said, pointing to a line awash in red ink, "money needed and no tax dollars to allocate. You're looking at over half a million dollars your school doesn't have—infrastructure repairs, athletic equipment, teacher salaries, all big-ticket items. Other things, like books and supplies, those are barely covered in the current budget, much less any increases for the future."

"Who knew textbooks were optional?" Merry rolled her eyes. "Obviously, we can't raise that kind of cash with a bake sale. Can we still save our high school?" She turned to Grady. "Can you?"

Grady closed the laptop and reached for her hand. "Merry, listen, I have an idea, but I can't do anything about it today. It's Christmas, but…"

"But…?"

"Dinner is served," Jane called from the kitchen. She carried a large turkey on a serving platter through the family room and placed it on the dining table. "Everyone, come eat."

"Hey, Daaaad," Trey yelled. "Food!"

A door upstairs opened and closed, and Artie came bounding down the stairs.

Arthur, wearing a cook's apron, appeared from the kitchen carrying dishes of steaming food. Savory smells emanated from the roasted turkey, fluffy white mashed potatoes, green beans sprinkled with almonds, buttered rolls, and pumpkin pie.

Merry's mouth watered.

Grady squeezed Merry's hand as he walked her to the table. "Let's enjoy the rest of Christmas, and I'll tell you my plan tomorrow."

On my birthday.

****

"Jane, that was delicious!" Merry plopped onto the sofa, propped her feet on the ottoman, and groaned as she patted her stomach.

The meal over, Arthur and Artie had taken Trey sledding, and Grady had gone back to his hotel. Just as Merry was about to doze off, she peeked open an eye to see Jane clearing dishes and silverware from the table. She pushed herself to her feet, collected a serving dish and platter from the table, and headed into the kitchen. "Where do you want these?" Merry glanced around the kitchen. She saw dirty cooking pots and utensils, leftovers that needed to be put into containers for refrigeration, and glassware that would have to be hand-washed.

"Now, Merry," Jane said with a hint of a *tsk tsk,* "I told you I don't ask my guests to pitch in."

Merry shrugged. "You didn't ask. I volunteered."

An hour later, the pots and pans were washed and returned to their cabinets; plates and eating utensils were in the dishwasher, and all leftovers had been safely stored away.

Merry glanced around the sparkling kitchen and nodded her approval of their work. "After eating too much of that delicious meal, it felt good to move around."

Jane dried her hands and hung the tea towel on a movable rack underneath the kitchen sink. "Eli told me tomorrow is your birthday."

"Eli?" Merry jerked to attention. "Did you hear from him today?"

Jane furrowed her brow. "Come to think of it, no. He mentioned a few weeks ago that you had a birthday the day after Christmas. I guess they had something in mind before…" She shook her head.

"Before their plans changed," Merry finished.

Jane brightened. "Ever been to a yoga class?"

Merry's eyes widened. "Not in a long time. Why?"

"I'm going in the morning. Work off some of this dinner. Care to join me?"

Merry shrugged. "Like I said, it's been a while. And besides, I didn't bring any exercise clothes."

"No problem. I'll loan you a pair of yoga pants. Any T-shirt will do. I'll get online and make the reservations. Class starts at nine, so we need to leave about eight-thirty."

Merry considered the impossibility, well, more like embarrassment, of attempting yoga poses after all these years, but she brushed aside that thought. Turning sixty was not an excuse to sit in a rocker. "It's a date."

Chapter Ten
Wednesday, December 26

Merry was determined to view December twenty-sixth as any other day. She got out of bed, drew aside the bedroom curtains for a look at the weather, which appeared to be a repeat of the day before, and instinctively checked her phone for a message from Robin. Still nothing. Disappointed, and now a bit worried, she headed into the bathroom.

An hour later, wearing a Belford Prep T-shirt and the bright-pink-and-blue yoga pants Jane left folded outside her bedroom door, she sat in the kitchen, checking and rechecking her phone while sipping coffee.

"Good morning, Merry. Happy birthday."

"I'd like to forget about that part." Merry set down her phone. "But thanks for…" She pointed toward the yoga pants.

Jane gave Merry's shoulder a squeeze. "Just remember. Sixty is the new forty."

"Ouch."

"Now, now, stop thinking like that." Jane gave Merry a visual once-over. "Look at you. Slender, healthy, attractive, no gray…"

"…thanks to my hairdresser…"

"No gray, however it occurs, and full of life and energy." Jane smiled. "Drink up, because we need to get on the road. The class is usually crowded, so if we want a decent spot on the floor, we need to stake out our spots."

Merry took one last sip of coffee, poured the rest down the sink, picked up her phone, and gave the screen one more glance. She slipped into her coat as she followed Jane into the garage, hopped into the passenger side of Jane's compact hatchback, and off they went.

****

Jane drove out of Irvington's historic district and wound her way through a more modern part of Indianapolis. She pulled into a strip center, with a large grocery store on one end, a karate studio at the other, and a bath and body boutique in the center next to Morning Star Yoga. She whipped into a parking space, popped open her trunk, and retrieved two yoga mats. Inside the studio, Jane slipped out of her snow boots, placed them in a row of cubbies along the side wall, and hung her coat on a hook.

Merry did the same. As Jane had predicted, the class was crowded the day after Christmas. *Probably a lot of overeating to atone for. Me, too.* The class consisted of ten other women, all about Robin's age, and two men who looked better suited for a game of pickup basketball than a yoga pose. She glanced around the small space and wondered how everyone would squeeze in.

An automatic diffuser spritzed something into the air that smelled like lavender mist, and loud, New Age-y music played.

The instructor, a tall, very slender, blonde woman about forty, tapped her watch, and adjusted the volume downward.

"Where do we go?" Merry whispered.

Jane pointed to a corner of the room near the wall.

Two of the other women adjusted their mats to give them space.

Once their mats were spread out, Jane retrieved two thick, foam blocks from a cabinet, one for herself and one for Merry.

The instructor sat at the front of the class, rang a bell, and thanked all the yogis for coming to the mat.

Merry squirmed as she looked at all the seasoned yoga students, feeling self-conscious about her lack of expertise, not to mention her unpainted toenails.

"You'll do fine," Jane whispered. "And if you even think about backing out, I'll announce to the class that today is your sixtieth birthday."

Merry gasped. "You wouldn't!" But a glance at Jane told Merry she would. So Merry twisted, turned, down-dogged, warrior-posed, and stretched muscles she hadn't felt in years. She finally caught her breath during the last few minutes as everyone relaxed on their mats, the instructor chanting about peace and love.

"*Namaste.*" The instructor bowed and rang the bell.

The music stopped, the lights came on, and everyone began rolling up their mats.

Jane stood to stretch her back. "I needed that." She glanced over at Merry. "And look at you. You're positively glowing."

"It's called sweat." Merry smiled in spite of herself. "Actually, I'm glad I came. But I can tell it's been a while." Turning sixty was a good reason to get moving again. She'd definitely look into joining a yoga studio when she got back to Belford.

They gathered their mats, returned the borrowed blocks, and stepped into boots and coats. Once they were ready to face the December chill, Jane fished her keys from her coat pocket. "If you liked that, wait till you see what's next."

Merry blinked. "Next?"

"When we get back to downtown Irvington. It's a haven of antique stores, coffee shops, and ghosts." Jane playfully nudged Merry. "Legend has it." She beeped open the car.

Merry slid into the passenger seat, almost too tired to fasten her seatbelt.

Jane started the car, cranked up the heat, and rubbed her hands in front of the vent.

Merry wrapped her coat tightly around herself, since the car's dashboard registered a frigid twenty degrees. Again, she pulled her phone out of her coat pocket to check for messages. Still nothing.

Jane backed the car out of the parking space. "You expecting a call?"

Merry was now very worried. It wasn't like Robin to not answer calls or texts. She glanced over at Jane. "Have you heard from the kids?"

"No, but I didn't really expect to." Jane winked. "It's sort of their honeymoon, you know."

Merry nodded. "I haven't heard anything from Robin for two days now."

Jane frowned. "Hmm. I haven't heard from Eli since they left Indianapolis on Christmas Eve. They had that layover in Denver, but Eli didn't text when they landed in Honolulu like he promised." She shook her head and smiled at Merry in the passenger seat. "I'm sure we'll hear from them today."

"I hope so, but it's just…"

"Just what?"

Merry barely knew Jane Beddington, yet for some reason she trusted her new friend. Of course, this concerned Jane's son as well. "Robin knows Christmas is a difficult time for me since her dad died. She and Eli are adults with their own lives, true, but not calling me on Christmas or my birthday is very out of character."

Jane's brow furrowed. "Perhaps we should check on their flight, to find out if it landed in Honolulu on time."

Merry now wished she'd done that two days ago. She poked at her phone and pulled up the airline's website. She swiped back and forth, looking for information on the flight her daughter was booked on. "I guess the airline updates their flights hourly, because there's nothing here from Christmas Eve. I'd need a computer to dig any deeper." She stared out the car window, lost in thought, as Jane retraced their route back to historic Irvington. Why no word from her daughter? If they'd missed their flight, surely Robin would have sent a text.

"Have you ever been down here?" Jane asked. "The historic shops in Irvington, I mean."

Merry snapped out of her head. "I've been to an amazing pizza place here and shopped in some of the antique stores, but it's been a while." She gazed out the window at Victorian-era storefronts with modern-sounding names, like Peterson's Coffee Emporium, Café Vic, Western Architectural Treasures, Mid-State Insurance, Irvington Theatre, and Bertha's Vintage Books. Merry could almost picture the hustle and bustle of the business and shopping district from a hundred years ago, sprinkled with antique cars or even a few horses and buggies.

Jane turned on her signal, yielded to an oncoming car on the busy, four-lane street, and pulled into an open parking space in front of Peterson's. An old-fashioned bell over the wooden door jangled as they walked in, the scent of fresh-brewed coffee, cinnamon, and pastries wafting through the small shop. Jane walked up to the counter. "Hi, Taylor. Hope you had a nice Christmas. Did Bella have fun?"

Taylor smiled, nodded, and smoothed down her green apron as she brushed a stray wisp of blonde hair off her forehead. "We did. It cost me a week's salary, but Santa was able to bring my daughter the historic replica doll she wanted. You?"

"We," Jane said, indicating her companion, "had a nice day, too. This is Merry Halliday, Eli's soon-to-be mother-in-law. She joined us for Christmas, and today…" Her eyes twinkled.

"Please don't," Merry said through gritted teeth.

"Today is Merry's birthday." Jane winked at Taylor.

Taylor beamed. "Awesome." She reached into the glass cabinet and retrieved two cinnamon crullers, placing the gooey pastries on porcelain plates. "Just out of the oven. Your usual beverage?"

"Yes, two orders." Jane tilted her head toward Merry. "And her money's no good here."

Taylor nodded, pushed two steaming mugs of chai tea across the counter, ran Jane's credit card, and then placed a lit birthday candle in one of the crullers.

Merry felt her cheeks turn crimson from all the unwanted attention. She mumbled "thanks" to Taylor and followed Jane to a table near the window overlooking the street. But they could have had their pick of any seat in the small shop, because they were the only customers. "Not many people out and about today." Merry removed her coat and draped it on the back of her chair.

Jane blew on her hot chai before taking a sip. "If I had to guess, I'd say the fine residents of Irvington are celebrating Boxing Day in the time-honored tradition." She winked at Merry. "You know, boxing up their unwanted gifts and returning them to the stores." She smiled at her own joke.

Merry smiled, too, because of course that's what Americans did on December twenty-sixth. Despite her intention of treating this as just another day with a fancy name, today was still that dreaded sixtieth birthday. If only she had no worries, and nothing better to do than spend hours in a shopping mall. Merry blew on her hot tea, took a tentative sip, set down the mug, and bit into the cruller, moaning with delight. She swallowed, picked up her mug with one hand, and checked her phone with the other.

This time Jane checked hers, too. "I'm now officially concerned. Eli always responds to my texts, even if it's nothing more than"—she put up air quotes—"K."

A ray of hope popped into Merry's head. "Has Grady heard from them? He mentioned he'd texted Eli."

Jane fired off a text, and her phone pinged back almost immediately. She shook her head with a sigh. "He says he's been working in his hotel room all morning and had his phone on Do Not Disturb."

Merry's mind conjured all kinds of horrors. What if Robin and Eli had lost their phones in transit and were now stranded with no way to contact their families? Or one of them was sick or injured and in the hospital? She shuddered. "Jane, do you think something's happened?"

Jane shook her head. "I think as moms we're entitled to be worried, but I'm not ready to panic." She drained the last of her tea and shoved it aside. "Still, we should go back to the B and B, get on the computer, and do some digging."

Merry nodded. She slipped into her coat, and they hurried out of the shop.

****

Jane carried her laptop to the dining room table and booted it up.

Merry paced back and forth behind Jane's chair.

Jane scrolled around on the airline's website. "Let's see what time their flight landed in Hawaii on Christmas Eve." She clicked around some more, hitting one dead end after another.

Merry pulled out her phone. "Go to the airline's home page so I can get their phone number." She glanced over Jane's shoulder, peered at the screen, and then punched the numbers into her phone. She got an automated answer and groaned when she was instructed to punch one for the status of departing flights, two for incoming flights, three for lost baggage, four for reservations, and five for customer service. She punched in the number five. "'Your call is very important to us yada yada yada'" she mimicked.

Merry waited, using up her battery life and her patience. "Can you try Grady again? Maybe by now…"

Jane nodded and fired off another text. Silence.

The knots in Merry's stomach got tighter the longer she was on hold with the airline. She continued to pace back and forth, phone to her ear, her imagination running wild as she pictured worse-case scenarios involving her only child. *No, don't go there.*

Jane's phone pinged with a text. She read it and glanced up at Merry. "It's Keith, and his message is somewhat cryptic. He says 'Everything is fine. See you at six p.m.' " Jane's brow furrowed. "What's that supposed to mean?"

Merry blinked. "Do you think he knows something bad and will only tell us in person?"

"I…" Jane started to say.

A human finally picked up her call and Merry held up a finger. "Yes, my name is Merry Halliday, and I'm checking the status of a flight my daughter, Robin Halliday, was on. December twenty-fourth. She and her fiancé, Elijah Williams, left Indianapolis and had a connection from Denver to Honolulu." Merry listened to the woman with the thick foreign accent. "But I…" She let out a sigh. "Yes, I'll hold." She rolled her eyes and slumped into a dining room chair.

"Well, at least you got through," Jane said. "Are you hungry? I can go make us some turkey sandwiches."

Merry was too keyed up to eat. "You go ahead, I'll…Yes, hello? I'm still here. I appreciate…Hello? Hello?" Merry blew out a huge puff of air and slammed her phone on the table. "I got disconnected! I spent half an hour on hold with customer service, and they cut me off."

Jane patted Merry's shoulder. "Why don't you go upstairs and rest a while? I'll try to get these elusive airline folks on the line, or at least get Keith to talk to me like a rational human being."

Merry started to object, but Jane's suggestion sounded reasonable. She was stressed out, her muscles sore from yoga, and she could use a soak in a hot bathtub. Besides, Grady had said something about six o'clock. She nodded and headed upstairs. She had to hope Grady had information to share about their children.

Chapter Eleven
Wednesday, December 26

Merry, wrapped in the B and B's fluffy pink bathrobe with a towel around her head, stretched out on the bed, relaxed enough from her bubble bath to close her eyes for a few minutes. Most of this day had been consumed with worry. Grady had information about the kids, so she planned to be up, dressed, and downstairs well before six o'clock when he arrived. *I'll just rest my eyes for a few...*

She awakened and realized she'd fallen into a deep sleep. A quick glance at the bedside clock told her it was already five minutes past six. She jumped up, tossed off the robe, and slid into her jeans and sweater. Her hair was still damp, so she finger combed it, stepped into a pair of loafers, and hurried out into the hallway. As she closed her door, she could hear muffled voices from below.

Maybe Grady is here. Maybe he knows what's happened to the kids. Merry took the steps two at a time.

"Happy birthday to you!
Happy birthday to you!
Happy birthday, dear, Mom/Merry,
Happy birthday to you!"

Merry stopped in her tracks on the bottom step, her mouth agape. There in the entry hall were Robin, Eli,

Jane, and Arthur, all singing at the tops of their lungs, while Grady harmonized. He held aloft a grocery store birthday cake alight with candles.

"Robin! Ohmigod, Robin!" Merry rushed over and threw her arms around her daughter. "Thank goodness. I've been so worried!"

"Sorry we worried you, Mom." Robin pulled back a bit and winked at Eli. "We had quite the adventure, but unfortunately, none of it in Hawaii. Since we couldn't finish our trip, we decided to fly back early and surprise you for your birthday." Robin linked her arm in Merry's and led her to the dining room table.

"Consider me surprised." She put her hand over her rapidly beating heart and patted Robin's arm while they walked. "Can you tell me…?" She shook her head. "I don't even know what questions to ask."

Grady set the birthday cake on the table. "Come blow out your candles. The details can wait till after cake and coffee."

Merry surveyed the cake and turned to Grady with a lifted eyebrow. "Six candles?"

Robin laughed. "It's symbolic, Mom. Plus that's all Jane had. Now make a wish and blow them out."

"I think my wish has already been granted, but all right." Merry took a deep breath and blew out the candles.

Arthur came out of the kitchen with plates, forks, mugs, and a carafe of coffee.

Eli did the serving honors, slicing the round chocolate cake with white icing into generous portions and carefully sliding each piece on a plate.

Grady, Jane, Eli, and Robin pulled out chairs around the oval dining table.

Arthur poured mugs of steaming coffee.

Everyone laughed, chatted, and enjoyed their dessert, while Merry offered a silent prayer of thanks for her daughter's safety.

"To Mom," Robin said, raising her coffee mug in a toast, "on her, uh, milestone birthday."

Merry winked at her daughter. "You can say it. Sixtieth. And I'm proud of it." She brandished her fork and popped an oversized bite of cake into her mouth.

"Hey, Merry, do you have any of those sugar cookies left?" Eli asked. "We went through that bag you gave us before we even got on the plane."

Merry shook her head and swallowed her bite. "I'm afraid Arthur's grandson polished off the last one."

"But you could bake more, right?" Jane said. "In fact, you *should* bake more. A lot more."

Merry blinked. "What?"

Jane leaned her elbows on the table. "Well, I've been meaning to ask you. We all love your cookies, more like we're obsessed with them, and I hoped maybe you'd be willing to sell them on consignment to our bed and breakfast guests," she said. "They don't have to be Christmas-themed."

Merry's eyes widened. "Seriously?"

Jane nodded. "They're that good."

Merry gave the possibility some thought. How would it even work? She still had her teaching job, or she hoped she did anyway, and Irvington was a considerable drive from Belford. But the idea excited her, and if she could figure out the baking time and transportation, maybe, just maybe...

"Think about it?" Jane prompted.

Merry nodded. The more she thought about it, the

more she liked Jane's crazy idea. "But now I have to know." She shoved aside her empty plate and turned to Robin. "What happened to you two?"

"First, a birthday gift," Robin said.

Merry lifted an eyebrow. "You already gave me a gift. The locket and the earrings." She patted the front of her sweater where her locket should be, reached to her ears that were devoid of earrings, and realized in her hurry to get downstairs, she'd left them all on the bathroom counter. "Oh, I…"

Robin shook her head. "This is just a token. And keep in mind there are limited choices in an airport gift shop." She pulled a small plastic store bag from behind the sofa and handed it to her mom.

Merry opened it and withdrew a T-shirt with the name of Denver's pro football team emblazoncd on the back. She giggled, set it aside, and dug into the bag again. Out came a gourmet chocolate candy bar, lip gloss, and a small empty picture frame.

"We're going to take a family selfie of the six of us, print it out, and put it in that frame." Robin hugged her mom. "I hope you aren't disappointed."

Merry's eyes watered. "Are you kidding?" She swallowed the lump in her throat and busied herself replacing the gifts in the bag. "After I didn't hear from you for two days, and all the things I was imagining, I'm just so relieved to have you here safe and sound." She sat straight in her chair and folded her hands in her lap. "Now, please tell me what happened."

"They called it a freak snowstorm," Robin began, "and that's saying something for Denver. Didn't you hear about it?" She shrugged. "Anyway, it was so bad that all the flights were grounded on Christmas Eve, and it even knocked out the airport's Wi-Fi and nearby cell phone towers. There were lots of stranded travelers, and no one had a way to contact anyone back home."

"But we met lots of interesting people from all over." Eli reached for Robin's hand and gave it a squeeze. "Houston, New York, Canada, and a young family flying to Hawaii like us."

Robin nodded. "We talked for hours with people we never would have gotten the chance to even meet, swapped stories about our favorite holiday memories, sang Christmas carols, and even played a game of dreidel. It was kind of magical."

Merry's brow furrowed. "You said you ate all the cookies. Is that all you had to eat?"

"Nope," Eli said. "The employees of a fast-food chain got stuck at the airport, too, so they fired up their grill, and Christmas dinner was burgers and fries."

"At first I was disappointed about our trip to Hawaii," Robin said as she released Eli's hand, "but then we realized we had a great story to tell."

"In a way," Eli mused, "it was a really special way to celebrate the holiday, all that unexpected camaraderie." He winked at Robin. "Every time our flight out of Denver was rescheduled, it was cancelled again before we could board. We didn't know when or if we'd make it to Honolulu, but then two seats became available on a flight to Indianapolis. We couldn't believe our luck."

"It was like it was meant to be, for us to come back home and surprise you on your birthday." Robin beamed.

Eli nodded. "I texted Dad just before we boarded the plane in Denver, and he picked us up at the airport this afternoon."

Merry glanced at Grady, who had been silent all this time, and realized what a lovely gift he'd given her for her sixtieth birthday. "Thank you."

Grady dipped his head. "And I have a gift for you as well. In a way."

"What? No! Just getting the kids here is gift enough."

Grady pushed out of his chair and grinned. "I think you're going to like this." He went to the coat rack near the front door, pulled a white envelope out of his jacket, and handed it to Merry.

Puzzled, she stood and paced back and forth as she opened it. Inside was a plain sheet of printer paper, on which he'd typed:

Hamilton Hardware Stadium

Muriel Peterson Memorial Foundation Auditorium

Gymnasium Scoreboard Sponsored by Meadows Advertising

Merry looked up from the page. "I don't get it."

Grady rocked back on his heels. "Remember I showed you that financial spreadsheet your principal sent me?"

Merry rolled her eyes. "How could I forget?"

"Well, after you and I talked about all the changes your school and students would undergo, it pricked my conscience. I wondered if I could just help fix the finances without my company taking over the school."

Merry frowned as she studied the page. "Okay…"

Grady reached across her and pointed to the paper. "This is just for your benefit. I'm working on a formal presentation for Dr. Alexander, your school board, and for Lake City Prep's board of directors. There was nothing I could do on Christmas Day," Grady reminded her, "but first thing this morning, I got on the phone with representatives from these three companies. They've agreed to buy naming rights to your school's football stadium, performing arts auditorium, and the gymnasium scoreboard. They'll be paying generously for those rights, too, for at least five years. You might still have to have that bake sale, but the naming rights money will allow Belford Prep to remain a community school and still get the needed repairs and improvements."

Robin's jaw dropped. "Mom, this is amazing!" She grinned as Eli high-fived his dad.

Merry was both stunned and elated and could barely contain her excitement. She reached over, impulsively gave Grady a big hug, and then pulled back, blushing. "I don't know what to say, except thank you. It must have cost you a great deal professionally."

Grady blushed, too, as he waved that away. "My star might not be rising at the moment, but it was the right thing to do." He pulled her back into his arms. "I did this for you," he whispered.

At Grady's touch, Merry felt another tingle go down her spine, and this time she knew why.

"Group hug!" Robin motioned everyone around her. She drew Merry toward her, Eli joined his fiancée, then took his mother's arm, and pulled her in as well. Grady and Arthur stepped in next to them.

Robin took out her phone. "Say cheese!" She snapped a selfie of the six of them. "That will go nicely in the gift shop frame."

Arthur sat at the piano and ran his fingers along the keys. " 'Happy birthday' or 'For He's A Jolly Good

Fellow'?"

"Both!" Merry shouted back.

Arthur's playing gave Merry a sense of peace and security she hadn't known in over three years.

I'm home.

Epilogue
One year later

"You ready, Mom?" Robin opened the door and stuck her head into the bedroom at Beddington and Breakfast.

Merry glanced around the room, the same one she stayed in a year ago. All the decorations were the same, but her life had changed so much. She gazed at her reflection in the mirror. With Paul's help, she'd chosen a beige, floral lace, mid-length dress that clung to her waist and flowed softly at her knees. The dress was sleeveless, so Paul insisted she add a shrug. After all, December was winter.

Robin came all the way into the room and stood next to Merry in front of the armoire mirror. "You look beautiful."

"You look pretty awesome yourself." Merry gave a nod to Robin's off-white, sleeveless sheath that clung to her baby bump in a most flattering way.

Robin surveyed her own reflection in the mirror. "I have to admit your friend Paul knows fashion. And by the way, happy birthday. The big six-one!"

Merry smiled. "Thanks."

"We gotta go," Robin said. "Jane's downstairs with the car warmed up, and everyone's waiting at the chapel." Merry and Robin hugged, and then descended the narrow staircase arm-in-arm.

Merry cast a quick glance into the combined living and dining room. It was all set up for the wedding reception—crystal wine flutes, china with gold trim, and a silver cake server tied with a white ribbon.

Paul baked a beautiful, three-tiered white cake with whipped cream frosting, topped with candy canes instead of a plastic bride and groom.

Next to the cake was a very large platter of Merry's sugar cookies, not only the Christmas shapes of stars, trees, angels, and Santas, but also bells coated with white-and-silver sprinkles, in honor of this day.

Jane's idea of selling Merry's cookies turned out to be very lucrative. In fact, the cookies had been so successful at Beddington and Breakfast, that when Paul opened his own bakery shop last summer, he asked if he could sell her cookies, too. Merry happily shared her grandmother's recipe, and with Paul's expertise, the cookies were big sellers.

Merry and Robin slipped into their matching winter white, full-length coats and hurried out the front door to Jane's car, sitting curbside with its engine running. Merry slid into the front seat, and Robin hopped in the back.

"Ready, ladies?" Jane asked.

"Ready," they both exclaimed.

The wedding chapel, a quick, two-block drive, was just as it had been a year ago when Merry and Grady had ducked in on Christmas Day. Their talk in the chapel that day inspired Grady to go the extra mile and help save her school. That generous act awakened Merry's heart and allowed her to fall in love with him.

A year ago, the chapel was empty except for the two of them, but today was a different day.

Inside the chapel, Jane handed Merry and Robin bouquets of white carnations.

At the minister's nod, Arthur, seated at the piano near the small altar, began playing the hymn she'd found last year, "This is a Day of New Beginnings."

Robin kissed her mother on the cheek. "Dad's smiling down on us," she whispered.

Merry nodded, even as her heart fluttered.

Robin walked ahead down the short aisle to stand opposite her husband Eli, who was serving as best man.

Merry stepped into the doorway and glanced around the chapel, a lump in her throat. The guest list was small, befitting the small venue. Of course, Jane, Arthur, his son Artie, and seven-year-old Trey were there. Merry's dear friend, Donna Ferguson, beamed and gave the bride two thumbs-up. Work colleagues Dr. Alexander, Coach Ralph Barrows with his wife Barb, and even Stefanie Summers were all present and smiling.

Kristina Timmons, now a college freshman with a volleyball scholarship, was also there. Last year after Merry confided her fear for Kristina's future to Grady, he got in touch with an orthopedic surgeon friend, and the doctor set Kristina's arm free of charge.

Merry's dear friends and neighbors, Paul Satterfield and Alex Gordon, sat near the front of the chapel. They brought guest of honor Spookie, who was perched on a satin pillow and sporting a rhinestone collar.

By the time Merry returned from her trip to Irvington last year, Spookie had already wormed her way into Paul and Alex's hearts. After a few futile attempts to bring her home, Merry realized Spookie *was* home with Paul and Alex.

She sold her condo. She and Grady recently closed on a condo of their own near downtown Indianapolis, close to the law firm where Eli practiced, and where Grady would soon join.

Belford Prep's improved finances had breathed new life into the faculty and student body. As happy as that made her, Merry only planned to commute to Belford for one more school year, and then retire and focus on her cookie business.

Grady tugged at his grey vest, adjusted the coordinating tie and beamed at Merry. Arthur hit a note, Grady opened his mouth.

Merry walked down the short aisle to the sound of Grady's rich baritone, singing the same song as beautifully as he had a year ago in this very chapel. She just knew Bert had a hand in her newfound happiness. She handed her bouquet to Robin and took a deep breath.

"Meow."

Everyone snickered at Spookie's approval of the nuptials.

"Dearly beloved," the minister said, "we're gathered here today to join Merry Carol Bell Halliday and Gradison Keith Williams in holy matrimony."

GRANDMOTHER'S SUGAR COOKIES

¾ cup Crisco—it's just not the same with butter!
2/3 cup sugar
2 eggs
½ tsp salt
1 tsp vanilla
1 ½ cups flour

Cream Crisco or butter, add sugar gradually, and cream together. Add eggs, salt, and vanilla. Lastly, add flour and mix well. Refrigerate at least an hour. Roll dough about 1" thick and cut with holiday-shaped cookie cutters. Bake on greased cookie sheet 375 degrees for 10-12 minutes. Cool, add sprinkles or icing. Makes about 36 cookies.

A word about the author…

Pamela Woods-Jackson is the author of six novels. She lives in Noblesville, Indiana (just north of Indianapolis) with two rescue cats, and she works part time at a living history museum.

Other Titles by this Author
Certainly Sensible
Confessions of a Teenage Psychic
Sole Mates
Teenage Psychic on Campus
https://www.facebook.com/pages/Pamela-Woods-Jackson/1523690337865060?ref=ay

Thank you for purchasing
this publication of The Wild Rose Press, Inc.

For questions or more information
contact us at
info@thewildrosepress.com.

The Wild Rose Press, Inc.
www.thewildrosepress.com

CPSIA information can be obtained
at www.ICGtesting.com
Printed in the USA
LVHW081251101122
732762LV00014B/887

9 781509 241941